C

"Well, we ——— **my new** ———

Luke grinned at Catherine with the predatory smile of a wolf in the fairy stories.
"We'll have to come to some little arrangement over the rent. Trouble is, I'm perennially short of the ready cash. Let's see now . . ." He looked at her consideringly.
"If only it were the other way around and I were your landlord, I'm sure we could agree on how you could, er, pay the rent."

Catherine felt the burning color leap to her cheeks as she jerked away from Luke's detaining arm. "Just get off my land, will you?"

"I was only going to say I'd be delighted to share my fold-up bed with you . . . if you were my tenant." Luke smiled lazily. "So don't be selfish. At least share your beach with me."

Rachel Ford was born in Coventry, descended from a long line of Warwickshire farmers. She met her husband at Birmingham University, and he is now a principal lecturer in a polytechnic school. Rachel and her husband both taught school in the West Indies for several years after their marriage and have had fabulous holidays in Mexico, Venezuela and Ecuador during revolutions and coups! Their two daughters were born in England. After stints as a teacher and information guide, Rachel took up writing, which she really enjoys doing the most—first children's and girls' stories, and finally romance novels.

Clouded Paradise

Rachel Ford

Harlequin Books

TORONTO • NEW YORK • LONDON
AMSTERDAM • PARIS • SYDNEY • HAMBURG
STOCKHOLM • ATHENS • TOKYO • MILAN

Original hardcover edition published in 1987
by Mills & Boon Limited

ISBN 0-373-02913-6

Harlequin Romance first edition June 1988

Printed in U.S.A.

CHAPTER ONE

THE man had the beach to himself. He leaned back against the rough trunk of the palm-tree, his slim, tanned fingers moving easily among the torn strands of the fishing-net, as though he had never done anything else in his whole life. But as his hands worked automatically his thoughts were sombre, his mind impervious to the dazzling beauty of the scene around him.

He was brought back to reality by the sound of a car. Shading his eyes against the brilliance of the late afternoon sun, he saw a battered-looking yellow Mini being driven rather too fast along the dusty track which led down towards the beach, leaving a white trail, almost like smoke, hanging in the still, clear air behind it.

The man's lips tightened in a grimace of annoyance. Earlier, he had heard the faint roar of the jet as it landed at the island's airport five miles along the coast, and now here was one of the beat-up hire cars from Sunshine Self-Drive, loaded with intoxicated tourists—drunk not only on excited anticipation of a Caribbean holiday but also with the generous tots of Courtesy Rum Punches which awaited every visitor arriving at the airport.

As he watched, the car slowed and then bounced to a standstill, half hidden from him by scrub and a thicket of pink oleander. He braced himself for a volley of slammed doors and raucous shouts, but there was only silence. The dust slowly began to settle, and he turned back to his net and his thoughts.

Catherine switched off the engine and, half closing her eyes, let her hands rest on the steering wheel. She

5

was, she realised, very tired. Between Heathrow and
Kingston she had been too restless to sleep, and had only
dozed off lightly after the plane had left Jamaica on the
final leg of the flight. She leaned back into the car seat,
feeling the intense heat, the vibrant colours, as always,
seep into the depths of her being. Through the open
window crept the familiar island smell—redolent at once
of lush tropical growth and insidious decay, and she
began almost imperceptibly to relax.

At last she reached forward reluctantly to turn on the
ignition, then stopped, her hand on the key. There was
no need to hurry on into town. Uncle Bob would not even
be expecting a reply to his letter for several days—
certainly not to see her, in the flesh, on his doorstep. She
smiled to herself, thinking of his face when he saw her.
He would no doubt scold her for her impulsiveness, but
she knew that his letter had given her the excuse she had,
almost unconsciously, been seeking to return to St
Hilaire. She caught sight of herself in the driving-mirror
and her smile faded as she guessed how Aunt Lu would
react to her pale, winter face, the dark shadows brushed
under her eyes like bruises, the faint dusting of freckles
across her nose only emphasising the pallor.

She reached for her sun glasses and as she put them on
she caught the glint of the sea through the undergrowth,
blue-gold. A bead of sweat was trickling slowly down
inside her white shirt-blouse and on a sudden thought she
knelt up on the seat and scrabbled in the small case
behind her until she found her blue and white gingham
bikini. Gratefully shedding the blouse and cream
gabardine skirt, which were clinging to her damp skin,
she wriggled into the bikini then surveyed her curves a
shade ruefully, thinking, Oh, those warming winter
puddings!

As she got out of the car she caught sight of a sign
hanging from a gnarled old cotton-tree. It was faded by
long exposure to tropical heat and rain but she could still

faintly make out the writing—and, in any case, she knew it off by heart: 'Coral Strand, one-fifth-acre plots for sale' and the name of a local real estate firm, while on a board held by one rusty nail was scrawled, 'All plots sold'. Some of the plots had in the distant past been marked out with metal posts and chains but these had now almost rotted away in the salty air.

A sudden shadow of pain darkened Catherine's eyes for a moment, but then she thrust her feet into her high-heeled leather shoes—quite unsuitable, but she wasn't going to risk stepping on a basking scorpion—and set off down the rough path which led away from the track through the scrub.

She rounded the final dense patch of undergrowth. The small pure white sand beach was a perfect shimmering crescent, curving at each end to a line of dark, jagged rocks, while in the distance, as though coming down to meet the sea, the line of pale blue-green wooded hills shimmered under the afternoon heat. Inshore, the water was a limpid turquoise-green which, further out towards the coral reef, deepened almost to violet.

Catherine's throat constricted and her eyes felt hot. I *was* right to come back, she told herself—this is where I surely belong!

At the far end of the beach was a group of palms and sitting in their shade was a man—one of the island fishermen, she presumed, although at this distance she couldn't recognise him. Years before, when her father had started his free night school for any of the illiterate adults of the island who wanted to learn reading and writing, the fishermen had come in a body and Catherine knew them all, by sight if not by name.

As she watched, the man raised his head and looked directly at her. She waved, but after staring briefly at her he bent his head to his work again. In that brief look, Catherine realised that he was a stranger, not a local, but

even so she was rather taken aback and for a moment the
sun seemed to lose its warmth. Then she shrugged. So
what? He wasn't in the mood for polite conversation, and
neither was she.

Without giving him another glance, she dropped her
sun glasses on to the sand, kicked off her shoes and ran
lightly down the beach; splashing through the milky
shallows, she struck out, revelling in the silken feel of the
water on her overheated body. She dived over and over
like a porpoise through the surging swell and came up,
gasping and spluttering. She tossed back her wet hair
from her face then, as she turned on to her back, she
sneaked a look across at the stranger. But he was stolidly
engrossed in his net, as though she didn't even exist.
Catherine was suddenly piqued; she knew that men
generally found her attractive and, although she was not
in the least conceited, this studied indifference stung her.

Her swim had brought her much nearer to his end of
the beach and she flipped over in the water, meaning to
swim back the other way. Then she stopped, a glint of
devilment in her eyes. Somehow or other, she thought,
she would get a response out of this man, if she had to
kick sand all over him to do it. She splashed out of the
water and walked up the beach towards his palm-tree,
scuffing her feet through the fine sand. As she came
nearer, though, her stomach fluttered nervously, for
there was a forbidding quality to him and, although he
must have been well aware of her, he continued to ignore
her, even when she came right up to him.

She stood looking down at him, her hands on her hips,
studying him curiously. His features were almost
completely hidden by the tattered straw hat tilted down
at a sharp angle over his face so that only the black,
shaggy hair and the firm, almost arrogant set of his
darkly stubbled jaw were visible. Almost against her will
she found herself watching as his slender, deeply
sunburned hands flickered in and out of the net, knotting

in the last broken strands of mesh.

At last, Catherine felt constrained to break the silence—indifferent on his side, self-conscious on hers—and she cleared her throat.

'Er—hello.'

'Hi.' Even now, he did not look up.

'Been having trouble with your net?'

She almost laughed out loud as she heard herself say the trite words, but at least they achieved some effect, for he slowly raised his head and his grey eyes subjected her to a very long, very deliberate scrutiny, taking in her oval face, wide-apart tawny-gold eyes, the toffee-brown hair clinging wetly to her neck and shoulders, and finally her rounded breasts and the curve of her hips. It was such a cool, unequivocally provocative look that Catherine recoiled, as though he had actually reached out a casual hand and caressed her, and instinctively her hands went up to her breasts in a defensive gesture.

She felt the angry colour flare up into her cheeks, but he had already turned back to his work, as if, well satisfied with the effect he had achieved, he was now contemptuously dismissing her. His whole demeanour was none too subtly warning her off, but Catherine had a stubborn streak in her a mile wide and she planted her feet firmly on the hot sand.

'You're not from St Hilaire, are you?' In spite of herself, the slight uncertainty came through in her voice.

'However did you guess?' His voice was sarcastic but there was no mistaking the accent.

'English, aren't you?'

'Could be.' There was a long silence, then he added, off-handedly, 'You're English yourself?'

At last Catherine had a chance to put him down. She gave a light laugh. 'Good lord, no—whatever gave you that idea?' she said, deliberately dropping her voice into the lilting island accent. But when he looked up at her sharply, she dropped her eyes in confusion. There was a pause, then she tried again.

'You're on vacation?'

'No.' His voice was curt.

'You mean you *live* here? Where?'

'Oh—around.' His expansive gesture, embracing half the Caribbean, increased her irritation even more.

OK, be like that, she thought.

Without looking at her, he remarked, 'By the way, you should be careful swimming here just now. We had a Norther blowing last week, and since then I've seen a couple of sharks inside the reef.'

Catherine's jaw dropped in astonishment. 'Well, thanks for telling me—now.'

'Oh, don't get excited—the sharks are so well fed in these waters, they're not likely to be over-interested in one slip of a girl.'

'Don't give me that old rubbish, please,' she snapped, forgetting the island accent. 'I was brought up with it. I never believed it when I was five, and I certainly don't now.'

'You were brought up—you mean, *you* live here?'

She carefully adopted his casual tone of a few minutes before. 'Oh, now and then,' she said with an off-hand shrug.

He seemed to lose the brief spurt of interest he had shown in her and, gathering up the net, got to his feet. Catherine watched him out of the corner of her eye as he uncoiled himself. While he was slouched up against the tree she had not realised how tall he was, and his brown muscular body showed a surprising grace of movement. But the tatty straw hat, the patched, sun-faded, hacked-off jeans, his whole casual demeanour, set him down as a beach-loafer—one of the many who regularly invaded the West Indies in search of the easy, lotus-land life of free sun, sand—and, she added ironically to herself, sex, when they could get it.

'I didn't realise you were a native. I took you for a tourist.'

His voice was cool, considering, and when she jerked her eyes up to his face he had tilted back his hat and was watching her. His face, in spite of the three days' beard, was full of lively intelligence and—yes—humour, sardonic certainly, but humour none the less. Somehow, she felt instinctively, this man was different—not at all like the loafers who, since her childhood, she had seen congregating outside the seedy downtown rum bars from early morning onwards.

As if he read her thoughts, his eyes became blank and his expression hardened again. 'Of course, you can't blame me. You haven't exactly got the island sun-tan—more of a dingy grey pallor.'

Deliberately he flicked his eyes critically over her body again and, quite suddenly, Catherine had had enough of this verbal sparring. She turned abruptly but he put a detaining hand on her arm and firmly drew her back towards him. He put a thumb under her chin to tilt her head up.

'Hmmm, pity about the eyes,' he murmured reflectively, as though to himself. 'I'd hoped you had soft melting brown ones to go with your hair—but you've got tiger's eyes.'

'Will you please let me go!'

Catherine tried to snatch her arm away but his hand tightened on it remorselessly.

'What's the matter? Peeved that I didn't immediately fall at your feet? I imagine that's what you're used to.'

Without warning, he cupped her chin in his hand, his fingers digging into her flesh. Too late, she realised what he was about to do and tried to wrest her head away, but his mouth came down hard on hers and then she tasted the saltiness of his lips and tongue. She tried to put up her hands to his chest to push him away but it was as though she was beating helplessly against a granite cliff. Only in

his own good time did he release her mouth, so that she
staggered back, panting, and would have sat down
heavily on the sand if he had not steadied her.

Her soft skin was tingling with the scratch of his beard
and her mouth was almost numbed by the bruising kiss,
so that for a few moments she was quite unable to get her
voice back and could only stand, glaring at him.

'Sorry about that,' he said, looking quite unrepentant.
'I just suddenly felt I had to take you down a couple of
pegs——' his eyes narrowed with amusement '—flouncing on to the beach as though you owned it.' Then, as she
still glared up at him, her eyes alight with fury, he
laughed. 'Don't take it so hard—at least you won't be
able to say you've never been kissed by a beach-bum!'

His voice was taunting but Catherine clenched her
fists by her sides, refusing to be provoked. Worthless—
worthless scum, that's all he is, she told herself fiercely, as
without a word she turned on her heel and walked away
up the beach, trying hard not to hear the soft, mocking
laugh that followed her.

At the far end of the beach she thrust her feet into her
shoes, hesitated, then risked a quick glance over her
shoulder. The man was in the act of rolling up his net. He
straightened and must have seen her but, as before, made
no sign as she retreated to the seclusion of the oleander
bushes.

By the time Catherine had slipped back into her blouse
and skirt—there was no need to take off her bikini,
which had virtually dried on her—and got back into the
car, her sense of humour had reasserted itself and she
smiled wryly. I knew I should have kicked sand all over
him, she thought—although Heaven knows what would
have happened if I had! Then she thought of his jibe—
'flouncing on to the beach as though you owned it'—and
at that she laughed out loud, as she started the car and
reversed fast down the track, back on to the road to town.

CHAPTER TWO

PORT CHARLOTTE was dozing peacefully in the afternoon sun as Catherine drove in, past the small, neat colour-washed duplex houses, each with its front porch overhung with trailing creepers. Down the side lanes, she caught glimpses of bougainvillaea—pink or peach-coloured, tumbling over yard walls, and occasionally the scarlet opulence of a poinsiana-tree. A few children were playing in the yards, and a brown mongrel dog appeared from the shadows under a veranda and chased the car half-heartedly, before flopping down again in the middle of the dusty road.

Almost without realising it, Catherine slowed as she passed the Public Hospital where her mother had worked as a midwifery sister. The hospital, which sprawled between the road and a marshy inlet of the sea, was exactly as she remembered it, except that today the walls were dingier than ever, the gardens even more neglected. No doubt, she reflected sadly, the interior was just as bad, despite her mother's constant battles with the Health Committee for more funds.

She drove on through the old quarter of town, parked, but still sat in the car. Nothing has changed, she thought, with a strange mixture of gladness and pain. Around the main square, the shops were just coming to after the long lunch-break. Young boys—the 'sprinklers'—were out, earning a few coppers watering the pavements, although the fine streams of water evaporated almost as they hit the ground. The small square was attractive in a down-at-heel fashion and many of the houses and shops still retained their faded shutters and delicate wrought-iron balconies—a French influence, left over from the days

13

before the British navy had pounded the French garrison into submission and withdrawal—while in the centre of the square, surrounded by bleached grass and a few dusty shrubs, there was a small pool and fountain commemorating one of Queen Victoria's jubilees.

The water from the fountain was splashing over the lip of the pool and, all at once, Catherine was reminded of the occasion, years before, when she and some of her classmates had jumped in, fully dresssed, for a dare, unfortunately just as one of their teachers drove past. The fact that she was the headmaster's daughter had not helped in the least—rather the contrary, she thought, smiling ruefully, as she got out of the car.

A few seconds' walk, and she turned under an archway into the courtyard of a colonial-type wooden house. Beside the heavy mahogany front door the brass plate read, 'Robert Latham, solicitor and notary public'. The door was ajar and Catherine, swallowing down the unwelcome lump that rose in her throat, went in, to be met by a blast of Arctic air-conditioning. Her arms covered in goose pimples, she quietly opened another door at the far end of the passage and put her head round.

A big, thick-set man of about sixty, with bushy grey hair, was sitting behind a desk, writing. As Catherine pushed the door open further he glanced up over his spectacles and his mouth dropped open.

'Good God—Catherine! I don't believe it!' Even after nearly thirty years, the blunt Yorkshire accent was still there.

'Yes, it's me, Uncle Bob.' She couldn't quite hide the faint tremor in her voice.

He pushed back his chair and came across to envelop her in a bruising hug, lifting her off her feet as though she were still ten years old. 'Wherever did you spring from? I thought you were still in London.' He released her, holding her at arm's length. 'And whatever have you been doing to yourself?'

'Oh, I'm all right, Uncle Bob—really I am.'

She smiled up at him reassuringly, but he clicked his tongue. 'I doubt whether your Aunt Lu will agree with you. You're so pale, and——'

'Oh, I'm fine.' Catherine was defensive. 'It's just the weather. I'm sure it's rained every day for the last two months, and you just wouldn't believe how cold it's been.'

'Oh, wouldn't I?' He laughed wryly. 'I seem to remember Leeds was always a bit short on tropical sunshine—although, heaven knows, I still miss the old place.' His face clouded momentarily but then another thought struck him. 'Did you get my letter before you left?'

'Yes, that's why I'm here. You said that something important might be coming up soon. Nothing more—just enough to whet my curiosity, and you know I could never stand mysteries. I hadn't started my research course, I was bored with my temping job, there was a seat on the next flight out—so here I am.'

Her uncle looked at her doubtfully. 'There really wasn't any need. Not yet, anyway——' But she interrupted him.

'Well, I have come, so what is this stupendous news? Not another of Aunt Lu's earth-shaking ideas, I hope!'

He laughed. 'Well, actually, she has been hatching a little scheme—and she might just be on to something this time. She's putting up a couple of self-catering cottages behind Cinnamon House, and she's got a few more ideas to cash in on what could be a mini-tourist boom on the island—and not before time, if you ask me. But no, it's not that. It's more to do with you. But I'm not sure whether——'

He paused, his blue eyes twinkling with mischief, and Catherine felt a twinge of irritation. She was, she reflected, too tired just now for any of Uncle Bob's teasing.

'Well, come on then—tell me.'

But he merely glanced at his watch and exclaimed with mock annoyance, 'I'm sorry, Catherine, but I've got to go across to Blue Bay—a dispute over the ownership of two nanny goats. But,' he went on hastily, as she looked ready to explode, 'as you've come all this way, perhaps I'd better spare you a few more minutes.'

He sat down again and gestured her to the chair facing his desk, paused for a moment to gather his thoughts, then said, 'You remember those little plots of land out near the airport that were for sale ten—no, fifteen years ago?'

Catherine stared at him perplexed. 'Coral Strand? Yes—I went—I drove past them just now.' For some reason, she was reluctant to mention her recent encounter on the beach. She smiled to herself in recollection. Her father had bought the plots for her birthday one year—almost, it had seemed, as a joke. She remembered them laughing over the price. What had it been—forty? No, fifty dollars apiece. Her father had shown the small Catherine a huge, awe-inspiring document and told her she was now in real estate, and that same day they had taken a photograph of her, standing on one of 'her' plots. She still had that photo somewhere . . .

She looked at him. 'Surely, no one's thinking of buying, are they? The land is pretty worthless—miles out of town, no mains water or electricity, just poor scrub that you couldn't even grow mangoes on.'

'That's as may be. But you're forgetting one thing—the beach, a perfect, small, untouched beach. And the owners of the land also have the waterfront rights.'

'So—OK,' Catherine shrugged, 'I can sit on my piece of beach for free—and maybe I could hire out sun-umbrellas to the thousands of tourists who don't go there every day!'

'Now, now.' He wagged a reproving finger at her. 'Just let me finish. For a start, you own twelve plots in all—that's two-thirds of the total area—and I own the rest.

Yes, it's true,' he went on, as she turned wide, disbelieving eyes on him. 'I recommended your father to buy in the first place—I could see the potential if no one else could. I told him it could well be a nest-egg for their old age, but he chose to buy them in your name.' He broke off and clumsily covered Catherine's slim hands with his own large paw. 'I'm sorry, pet. It's hard for you, very hard, I know.'

He squeezed her hand and gave her a lop-sided smile. 'It's always hardest for those who are left. Lu and I lost the best friends anyone could wish for, and you lost the best parents in the world.' As Catherine's hands moved convulsively, he tightened his grip on them. 'You know we weren't able to have children, Lu and I, but you've always been like a daughter—or, at least, a favourite niece—to us, and since then, even more so.'

She forced a smile and returned the pressure on her hands. 'I know, Uncle Bob, and I'm grateful—more grateful than I can ever say. But you're not to worry about me. I've got over it, really I have. After all, it's over four years ago now.'

She managed another reassuring smile, but then was silent for a moment, remembering . . . the headmistress gently telling her the shattering news of the accident . . . matron taking care of her as the terrible, bleak greyness settled over her . . . then, Bob and Lu arriving, having rushed to England on the first available plane. As her guardians, they had quietly taken control, seeing to the funeral and the thousand and one awful things that had to be done, smoothing away difficulties as if by magic to ensure that she was financially secure, could finish her education and, above all, keep Hope's Mill, which was what she had most desperately craved to do, as though, by keeping the beloved home, somehow she would keep a tangible link with her parents. They had comforted her, loved her, helped her to come through a nightmare so horrible that at first it had seemed to her that she herself would hardly be able to survive it . . .

She looked across at him steadily. 'You must just let me
say this, Uncle Bob. I shall never be able to repay what
you've done for me—no, let me say it,' as he tried to brush
her words aside, 'not in a million years, but I shall never
forget—never.'

Catherine broke the silence that followed her words by
reaching for her bag. 'And now—you'd better not keep
those nanny goats waiting any longer! And besides, I
must get off to Hope's Mill. I rang Mattie from the
airport.' She grinned at the recollection. 'Poor Mattie—I
gave her quite a shock, but she's no doubt scurrying
around now, looking for imaginary dust!'

'But you must stay with us while you're here. You'll be
lonely out there all on your own.'

'Mattie will be there—and, anyway,' she gave him a
steady smile, 'Hope's Mill is my home.'

'Well, at least come to dinner tonight, or I'll never hear
the last of it.'

'Yes, I'd love to—but now I really must go.'

'Don't rush off quite yet, Catherine. I still haven't told
you quite everything.' He picked up his pen and rolled it
reflectively through his fingers. 'You've heard of
Brannan International, the hotel chain? Well, they're
interested—*extremely* interested—in Coral Strand!'

Catherine stared at him, her tawny eyes widening with
stupefaction. 'But—they wouldn't want to come to St
Hilaire. They go to places like Jamaica—or the
Bahamas. The hotels that are here already are more than
enough to cope with the visitors we get. In England,
when I tell people where I come from, they say, "Oh,
yes," meaning "Where the heck's that?" No one's ever
heard of this place. You're having me on—or someone's
having a joke at *your* expense.'

He laughed shortly. 'Multi-million-dollar companies
don't joke, love. Their time's too valuable to waste
laughing. No—it's true. Their chief surveyor, who was

down a couple of months ago, told me—in confidence—
that they want to get in on an undeveloped island. People
are always going on about "small is beautiful"—well,
that goes for islands as much as anything else,
apparently, and they like the quiet, old-fashioned feel of
this place.'

'But if a big hotel chain like that moves in, how long
will it stay that way? I don't want to be a hypocrite, and if
we do sell the land, that's marvellous, but can't we try and
find a local—or, at least, a West Indian—buyer? That
would at least ensure that most of the money stays on the
island.'

She stopped suddenly, surprised by the expression that
flickered momentarily across Uncle Bob's face. 'If there
were any locals interested, they could have made an offer
years ago,' he said. 'Besides, there are plenty of
unemployed on the island since the sugar-cane market
hit hard times, and they're not going to share your
qualms, I'm sure. Anyway, don't you want to know what
they're offering?'

Catherine's eyes were fixed on his face but her
thoughts were racing away at top speed. It was a pity that
her beloved Coral Strand should be sold to outsiders, but
her uncle must be right. He had so much business sense,
and besides ... if the price was high enough, she
could ...

'What would you say to twenty thousand? That's US
dollars, of course.'

'Twenty thousand dollars—that's wonderful.'

'That's for each plot, of course. So, you should net—
oh, a quarter of a million dollars, if the deal goes
through.' He laughed. 'Oh, Catherine—if you could see
your face! But,' he held up a warning finger, 'we must
keep all this absolutely to ourselves until it's settled.
Things are a bit sticky over outside development just
now, so I want to present it as a finished package—local
building contractors, local materials, long-term employ-

ment et cetera. But do remember, we haven't landed the big fish yet—absolutely nothing's settled.'

Catherine leaned back and sighed luxuriously. 'Oh, there's no hurry. I can wait—I might even have got used to the whole idea by then. And it's marvellous, because it gives me the chance to——'

'There's just one little hitch which I suppose I should warn you about.'

She frowned slightly. 'A hitch?'

'Yes. That's why I didn't say any more in my letter—I was waiting until it was all finalised. But—you see, you've got a squatter.'

'A squatter?'

In the area round her dingy flatlet in London, squats were quite a common occurrence, some of them ending in violence as the unwelcome guests were evicted. But here? On St Hilaire? No—it was too ludicrous.

'Yes, and I'm afraid he's chosen one of your plots to ensconce himself on. I've been dealing with him, representing myself as the solicitor of the principal concerned—which of course I am. I said, why the hell doesn't he go and squat somewhere else, but he says he likes the view from Coral Strand.' Mr Latham's face darkened in anger. 'Of all the no-good, insolent layabouts I've ever——'

'But who *is* he?' Catherine demanded.

'His name's Devinish—Luke Devinish. But that's just about all anyone knows about him. He arrived out of the blue a couple of months ago on a boat, which he immediately sold—no doubt to fill his skin full of white rum. Now he's got an old dinghy, does some fishing, takes tourists out to the reef, just like any of the local fishermen. Funny thing is, everyone seems to like him— especially the women. Even your aunt's got a soft spot for him.' He scowled. 'He's got quite a little sideline going, selling her bits of fancy driftwood to decorate those bungalows of hers. I don't know what the world's coming to, I really don't. We could *all* opt out—*I* could sit under a palm-tree all day long, scratching myself.'

Catherine was still laughing when a sudden, appalling thought killed the smile on her lips. Oh no, she thought, no, don't let it be—please!

'Th-this squatter. He's American, I suppose?'

'No—he's as English as we are. Not that he's ever condescended to tell anybody, but his accent's English enough—when he deigns to speak.' He sighed. 'Anyway, that's it, I'm afraid. He's there, and he informs me he's every intention of staying.'

'Oh, has he?' Catherine's normally good-natured face was flushed with annoyance. 'Well, he's just going to have to change his mind! And surely there's no problem. It's my land—so OK, I'll evict him, and he can go and squat somewhere else, like five hundred miles away.'

'But it's not quite as easy as that, love.'

She looked across at his rather weak, worried-looking face and sighed inwardly. Bob Latham was an easy-going man, who wanted only to live peaceably with all the world and was perpetually being astonished when this proved difficult or impossible.

'Of course it's easy, Uncle,' she said firmly. 'I appreciate that maybe you couldn't do much, as he's actually on *my* land, but as of now I'm authorising you to contact the police and get that man off—and I don't much care how they manage it!' She realised that her uncle was staring at her in surprise. She herself was taken aback by the violence of her reaction. Would she be feeling quite this way, she asked herself, if she had not already met her non-paying guest—and she was quite sure that she had—and come off very much second-best from the encounter? She shivered at the memory as she felt again the ruthless insistence of his lips against hers.

'I want that man off my land,' she repeated stubbornly, but he shook his head.

'I wish it were that simple but you see, he has certain rights.'

'Rights? How can a squatter have any rights?'

'Normally, he wouldn't have. But in this case . . . You remember the island history you did at school, Catherine? The 1842 Protection of Land Rights Act?' He waved a hand towards a set of old leather-bound books on a shelf. 'I'll find it for you if——'

Catherine groaned. 'No, there's no need. My O level History's coming back to me, more's the pity. ". . . and that no emancipated slave, or other personage, may be summarily evicted from uncultivated land . . . blah, blah . . . whereon he has erected a dwelling and has made smoke to rise from the hearth of that same dwelling——"'

'"——within the space of twenty-four hours." That's it. I always told your father you'd make a good lawyer. What a waste, doing English Literature——'

She brushed this aside impatiently. 'And did he? Did he get the dwelling up, and smoke from the hearth in twenty-four hours—or can we get him on that?'

'Oh, he managed it all right. Used wood from a wreck along the coast to make a rough cabin among the scrub behind the beach, then got the fire going. Funny though—him being English, how the hell did he know about this loophole?'

'Oh, good things like that get around the drop-outs' grape-vine,' Catherine said sourly. She suddenly smacked her fist down on the desk so that the china beaker of pens leaped. '*Why* did he have to come to this island? And *why* did he have to choose *my* land?'

'Now, don't get yourself in a state again, love. I've already started the process of taking him to court. With a sympathetic judge, we should win—that clause should have been taken off the Statute Book years ago. It was never intended for a case like this. And anyway, I can't see him staying for long. One of these days, he'll get bored, then he'll be up and away to another palm-tree, another beach.'

'Oh no, he won't.' Catherine's laugh was bitter. 'He's been here what—two months? There's nothing to prevent him staying two years—or twenty. I can just see him like some horrible Ancient Mariner still squatting on my land, and I'll point him out to my grandchildren and say in a quavery voice, "Look there, my darlings—that evil, hairy, old reptile——"

Her uncle broke in reprovingly, 'Don't let that vivid imagination of yours run away with you, chuck. Be patient, for a little while. There's no frantic hurry, as I told you.'

Catherine made an effort to control herself. 'Perhaps the Brannan company will be prepared to buy with a sitting tenant, then chuck him off?'

'Oh, no.' To her chagrin, he sounded almost shocked. 'No—I mentioned him to the surveyor—thought I'd better—and he said to make it worth the man's while somehow to leave, but do it legally. Old man Brannan's a stickler for the law, apparently—he's a lawyer himself. But he also made it very clear that as long as the fellow stays, there's no deal. On an investment of this size, they're not going to take the slightest risk of their plans falling through.'

'Well—we'll offer him money, then. That's all that type are interested in—a year's rum money should do it, surely?'

'I've already tried that, I'm afraid, when this scheme was first mooted—without letting on to him, of course. If he should find out what's in the wind—and it's absolutely vital that he doesn't—that will only make him all the more awkward. Anyway, he told me what to do with the money—or words to that effect. What he really meant, I suppose, was that he was setting out to be as cussed and bloody-minded as he could be.'

'I can imagine,' Catherine said drily. With a few deft

strokes, her uncle was certainly painting a Rembrandt-like portrait of the man on the beach. It would be quite some undertaking, she acknowledged grimly, to force *him* into something he didn't choose to do. But somehow or other she would do it. Her soft lips were set in a firm line and she went on with renewed fierceness, 'I'll get rid of him—somehow—I promise you!'

He laughed and ruffled her head affectionately. 'That's my little pussy!'

But she shook her head at him. 'No, I mean it. Even if—even if I have to drag him and his cabin bodily down the beach, I'll get him off my land—if it's the last thing I do!'

'Well, if you're sure you don't want anything, Miss Cathy, I'll be off to bed now.'

Catherine smiled up at the stout, dusky-skinned woman and gave her hand a quick squeeze. 'Thanks for waiting up for me, Mattie. And thanks for looking after Hope's Mill so well—and everything.'

'Go along with you, it's my job. Now don't you sit up long, either. You look real peaky.'

Catherine nodded and smiled affectionately at her retreating back, then settled herself in the cane chair. She really should take Mattie's advice, she knew, but she just wasn't ready for sleep. Although she had put on a brave face to Uncle Bob, coming back to Hope's Mill had been an ordeal, but she had faced it and perhaps now the worst was over. Her gaze wandered past Port Charlotte, laid out before her in the tropical moonlight, to the lush hillsides beyond and the clear outline of the Academy where her father had been headmaster. Quite deliberately, she allowed her thoughts to stay with the past . . .

At first, they had lived on the school campus but then her father, always impetuous, had bought Hope's Mill. Isolated among the plantations of sugar-cane, it was a pleasant, rambling stone house, all creaking floorboards and high-louvred window frames, which had once been the estate foreman's quarters. In the garden behind the house was the eerie, roofless shell of the old sugar-boiling house, while among the rich tropical foliage the stone piers which still stood astride the cascading stream were all that remained of the huge water-wheel.

Yes, Catherine reflected, they had all been so very happy at Hope's Mill, she in particular, with the vivid, intense happiness of childhood, which does not allow for even the remotest possibility of change. The first blow had fallen when she was just sixteen and her father had insisted on sending her away from the island, to boarding-school near London. And then, after her parents' deaths on that recruitment trip to England during her first year there, she had felt quite unable to return to St Hilaire.

With a variety of excuses, she had evaded the pressing invitations of Bob and Lu, and had deliberately chosen to go to university in England, rather than to the University of the West Indies or a college in the States, with friends she had known since her earliest schooldays. But that period had passed and for some time now, with increasing certainty, she had hugged to herself the thought of once again taking up those friendships and ties. In the darkness, Catherine smiled wryly as she recalled how, over dinner, listening to Aunt Lu's warm island voice, her dream had crumbled to dust.

'. . . and Julia's working in a hospital in New York . . . the McLellan twins—they're both in Canada . . . oh, and Lorna's up in Miami with Lance, while he completes his law studies—she's expecting a baby soon.'

Catherine had stared at her aunt, almost aghast. Lorna—the first and closest friend since the five-year-old Catherine had faced those bewildering days in a new school, a new country! Aunt Lu's unwitting words had given her a strange feeling of unease. She had held Port Charlotte in her mind, unchanging, but she realised now that it was she who had stepped off the fairground ride, she who had been left behind . . .

It seemed that only one link remained to tie her to the past. Just as she was leaving, Uncle Bob had said, in a too-casual voice, 'Oh, by the way, Cathy, Nick Alvarez is back. Now there's a young man who's done well for himself—when his mother died, he was off to Venezuela with hardly a pair of shoes to his name. Now he's got a house up on the Heights, a yacht that he charters, and he's bought a bar on the waterfront and done it up like an English pub. Beer pumps, horse brasses, the lot—calls it the Lord Nelson. It's a little gold-mine.'

Nick back . . . In spite of herself, Catherine's heart beat a little faster. Nick—so handsome that all the girls were wild for him, while Catherine, shy and young for her age in comparison with the island girls, encumbered—or so she thought—with puppy fat and those huge eyes, like some strange tawny animal, had been left behind—until that night of the end-of-term party, when at last he had taken notice of her . . .

She knew suddenly why she was so restless. It wasn't just coming back to Hope's Mill. She wanted to see Nick—now, tonight. *He*, more than anyone, would surely banish the unwelcome recollections of the man on the beach, which were continually intruding on her mind. Without giving herself time for rational thought, she snatched up her bag and, coasting the car down the slope so as not to disturb Mattie, drove back towards town.

Nick back . . . Her uncle's voice was replaced by another, as she remembered how she had overheard her father—'. . . a very impressionable age . . . that wild, unprincipled, *dangerous* young man . . .' just before he told the pale, distraught Catherine that she was being sent to school in England . . .

It was impossible to miss the Lord Nelson. What Catherine remembered as a seedy, half-derelict bar in an

eighteenth-century warehouse on the banana wharf had
been transformed into a sparkling black-and-white-
timbered pub, complete with its authentic-looking sign
hanging above the entrance. She parked and, not
allowing herself time to reconsider, followed a group of
young tourists inside. A raucous blast from a steel band
met her ears, while the thick blue haze of smoke made
her blink, and for a few moments she stood, her eyes
gritty with fatigue, feeling, This is ridiculous, I shouldn't
have come . . .

'Good Lord—Cathy? Catherine Hartley?' Nick
Alvarez thrust his darts into the board and pushed his
way across to her. He seemed much older than her
myriad memories of him—polished and even more
handsome. 'Well, well—little Cathy.' He smiled down at
her, that crooked, conspiratorial smile that a few years
earlier would have turned her legs to water. 'You've
grown up, little Cathy.' His eyes flicked down her body
then back to her face.

'Hello, Nick.' She smiled up at him, unable quite to
keep the surprise out of her voice. The casually expensive
shirt and slacks, the heavy gold signet ring and chunky
gold bracelet watch—this was not the Nick she remembered.

'Yes,' he went on reflectively, still holding her hand,
'you've certainly grown up.'

He gave her a slanting smile and Catherine, feeling her
cheeks grow warmer, said quickly, 'Not before time, I
should think! I was very podgy—and very innocent.'

'Oh, surely, that was the added spice.' His eyes glinted,
'And now—well——'

He cupped her face between his hands and she caught
the faint sweet smell of rum on his breath, but even as his
mouth came down towards hers she stiffened with shock
and his kiss landed on her cheek. Her eyes, sliding past
Nick's shoulder, had focused, among the blur of
unfamiliar faces, on one that she recognised only too

well. Luke Devinish was standing in the doorway. He was in the same faded denim shorts and a shabby pale blue shirt, yet Catherine, wanting desperately to despise him, realised to her chagrin that he made every other man there, including Nick, seem overdressed.

His eyes flickered across her face with a momentary expression of contemptuous hostility that made Catherine feel for a moment as though he had struck her, then it was replaced by the same careless indifference she had encountered on the beach. He came into the room and thrust past her so that, caught off balance, she lurched against Nick, who put his arm round her waist and drew her close to him.

'Hey, Luke, man—don't you go pushing my girl about!'

But he ignored Nick, and went over to the bar.

'Oh, Nick surely you don't let people like that in here!' Catherine exclaimed.

He shrugged. 'I'm in this business to make money, Cathy—lots of lovely money. As long as he can pay for his drink, he's welcome. Don't upset yourself over him, honey. He's not worth it.'

Nick steered her to an empty table and, despite her protests, shouted to the barman for two rum punches. She leaned back against the wall, sipping her drink and watching him, showing off slightly in his role of 'mine host'—hurling repartee across to a group gathered round the dart-board, and being kissed enthusiastically by a couple of gorgeous blondes in skin-tight bermudas who floated past their table.

The steel band was playing a slow, dreamy 'Fly Me to the Moon' and Nick pulled her to her feet. The dance-floor was a small open-air patio illuminated only by a string of fairy lights. Catherine went rather stiffly into his arms but he held her close and after a moment she allowed herself to relax against him. Eyes closed, she remembered the last time she had danced with him—the school dance, when she had at last persuaded her mother to let her wear a more grown-up dress and put up her heavy fall of hair, leaving her neck and shoulders bare. And Nick, two years older, had looked at her as though noticing her for the first time. Then, as now, he had held her suffocatingly close as he danced with her—and she fell headlong into the pains of adolescent love . . .

The music had ended. Catherine opened her eyes and drew back from Nick's arms. She smiled up at him, finding it difficult for a moment to quite focus on him.

'I really must go, Nick, I'm sleepwalking.'

She turned, slightly unsteadily in the half-dark, and collided heavily with something bulky and unyielding, so that she stumbled and would have fallen had she not been caught sharply by the elbows. Instinctively, she put her hands up against the man's chest and felt against her outstretched fingers his heart beating under the thin shirt.

'I'm sorry. It was my fault——' she began, but the words died on her lips.

'That's all right, lady. Feel free to break the other foot next time.'

She dropped her hands from his chest as though it were red hot, as Nick exclaimed with mock anger, 'Hey, Luke, I've told you—leave my girl alone! You OK, honey?' And when she nodded dumbly, he said, 'Here's your bag. I'll see you to your car.'

Outside, Catherine turned to him. 'It's been great to see you again, Nick, and I'm so glad you're doing so well—your Mom would be proud of you.'

She held out her hand, and he took it and kissed it. 'You're a lovely girl, Cathy. Take care.' His voice was serious for once and Catherine, half of her still in the past, smiled at him tremulously.

'See you, Nick.'

But as she drove away, her heart was sad. She had known, almost from the first moment of meeting Nick again, that there was nothing left, not the remotest vestige of her girlish passion for him; the ghost of the past was laid. Now, there was only affection for the Nick who was a part of that past. She had been away too long . . .

She parked the car and walked slowly up the veranda steps. Lorna—married . . . to Lance, whom she had adored for years . . . pregnant—and blissfully happy, no doubt . . . Carole . . . Angie . . . Julia . . . everyone gone . . .

She showered and collapsed into bed, worn out by a blend of physical exhaustion and a disturbing feeling of anti-climax. Through the pale shroud of the mosquito net she caught sight of her wan, heavy-eyed self in the mirror. Her last conscious thought was of Nick. But it was not *his* face that she saw just before she plunged into an abyss of sleep—it was a thin, darkly arrogant face, the cold grey eyes watching her with an implacable hostility.

CHAPTER THREE

'WHOAH, Pepe! Good boy.'

Catherine pulled hard on the reins, controlling the frisky animal with difficulty, and for the umpteenth time blessed the party of cruise-liner tourists who had hired all of Mr Brownlow's sedate plodders, leaving her with only this superb but highly-strung animal. The dry stems of sugar-cane rustled all around them in the hot breeze from the mountains and Pepe pricked his ears at the sound, whinnying with impatience. Catherine had intended returning the way she had come but below her the sea shimmered blue-green in the late afternoon sun, tempting her down.

She clicked her tongue. 'Come on, Pepe, let's go.'

Once down on the shore, she at last allowed the horse to canter until, rounding a rocky outcrop, she pulled him up suddenly, her lips tightening. She had completely forgotten that this route back to the stables lay past Coral Strand, and now they were almost there. She sat, chewing her lip, as she tried to decide what to do. They could return the way they had come—a long, hot, uphill ride. They could follow the main road—not a good idea with such an unpredictable horse. Or——

Catherine scowled in the general direction of Coral Strand and shaded her eyes with her hand, straining to see if *he* was anywhere to be seen, then aloud she said angrily, 'Oh, what the heck! It's *my* beach—and ten to one he'll be asleep under one of *my* palm-trees!'

But even as she spoke, she saw a figure by the water's edge, dark against the white sand beach. If she had allowed herself to hesitate, Catherine might well have turned the bridle meekly in the opposite direction. But

31

there was something about that distant figure . . . She
jammed down her riding-hat and lightly touched Pepe's
flanks with her heels.

'Come on, boy, let's show him what we can do.' And
they took off, galloping through the white foam which
rippled up the beach, scattering a cloud of sea birds from
under his very hooves and leaving shining droplets of
spray bursting behind them. Bent low over Pepe's back,
laughing aloud in almost reckless abandon, Catherine
saw the man straighten up and shade his eyes to look at
them, then turn his back and begin to walk away up the
beach. The calculated indifference caught her on a raw
nerve. She clicked her tongue to Pepe and he almost flew
under her. Out of the corner of her eye she glimpsed the
man as he stopped and slowly turned to watch them
tearing along the beach, tossing up the sea behind them.
She knew that she was showing off but, caught up in the
exhilaration of the moment, she didn't care . . .

Just ahead of them, at the far curve of the beach, was
the line of jagged rocks. She pulled on the reins and
slowed slightly to turn Pepe away from the water's edge.
It was that loss of speed that saved them both, for
Catherine had forgotten, until she was almost upon it,
that just beyond the rocks was an old concrete groyne
running down into the sea. It was low enough for the
horse to take it easily but even as he gathered himself to
spring, she saw with a lurch of fear that on the far side the
sand had been washed away, so that the level dropped by
several feet. Pepe landed heavily on the uneven ground,
one hoof caught in a land crab's burrow, and, unable to
save herself, Catherine tumbled awkwardly out of the
saddle.

As she lay on the damp sand, winded and furious with
herself, she heard an angry exclamation, then running
footsteps. Leaning back, she watched with resignation
from under her long lashes as he vaulted over the groyne
and came towards her. His shadow fell across her and she

closed her eyes, bracing herself for the withering comments as he helped her up. But nothing happened and, opening her eyes again, she saw almost with disbelief, that, ignoring her presence completely, he had gone to Pepe, who stood sweating and trembling.

Catherine's feelings of foolish embarrassment evaporated in a slow surge of anger which temporarily robbed her of any ability to move, so that she continued to sprawl inelegantly on her back as he gently soothed the horse until Pepe relaxed and stood quietly. Then he knelt on the sand and ran his fingers slowly and efficiently up and down the animal's legs, finally standing up again to brush the sand off himself.

Without even looking at her, he said, 'Well, he's strained a fetlock, but be grateful it's nothing worse.'

'Oh, I'm *so* glad,' she replied with heavy sarcasm. In reality she felt weak with relief but it did seem, she thought resignedly, that every time she came within a hundred yards of this man, her natural friendliness disappeared under a new wave of antagonism.

He shot her one cold glance then, without looking at her again, began to stroke Pepe's nose.

'No thanks to you.' His voice was curt. 'You could have killed him or maimed him for life, you little halfwit.'

Later, Catherine thought, when she had escaped from Coral Strand and this loathsome man, she would allow herself to feel weak with gratitude that neither of these things had happened, but now she could only respond to the angry derision in his voice.

'Oh, good. Of course, *I* might have——'

'I can't understand Brownlow letting a child like you get astride Pepe. No, don't tell me——' he held up an imperious hand to silence her as she began to protest angrily '—of course, it was that lad of his. Henry was no doubt the worse for rum again this morning!'

How dared he! Mr Brownlow was a dear—easy-going,

kind, endlessly patient when the ten-year-old Catherine was learning slowly and painfully to ride. The angry colour flared in her cheeks and she gave a disdainful laugh.

'I'm sure you're a great one to talk about people drinking too much—you never do, I'm quite sure.'

'That's right. I don't.'

He slipped Pepe's reins over the whitened stump of an old logwood-tree then, without even a glance at her, walked away up the beach with quick, easy strides. With a groan, Catherine eased herself up into a sitting position. God, what a man! she thought. What a perfectly vile, unbearable brute. She watched as he disappeared into a small, makeshift-looking hut set back among the tangle of scrub. So that was it! Home Sweet Home—the packing-case residence which, unless she was very careful, was going to deprive her of a fortune.

Her lips were tight as he came back, holding an old shirt. Still ignoring her, he set to work, deftly tearing it into long strips and bandaging Pepe's fetlock tightly while Catherine, against her will, found herself covertly studying him. The powerful shoulders, long legs, slim hips—it was a superb athlete's physique which didn't, in the least, she thought sourly, need expensive clothes. In fact, the faded denim shorts somehow enhanced instead of detracting from his appearance. His face was turned away from her and as she watched he brushed his hair impatiently back from his eyes and stood up. He had the same easy grace of movement as a panther prowling behind its bars—and the same coiled tension, she thought with a sudden pang of fear, that could make him very dangerous if he were pushed too hard. She swallowed and forced her eyes away from him.

'Come and hold his head—he's a bit restive.'

When she didn't at once reply he repeated his terse command.

'Oh, so sorry,' she said icily. 'Were you speaking to

me? I thought you were talking to something that had crawled out from under that stone.'

Watch it, my girl, she told herself, keep a hold of your temper. But all the same, it was very difficult—his total and, she was sure, deliberate indifference to her got under her skin far more than ordinary rudeness could ever have done. At least you knew where you were then, she thought with a slight tremor, whereas with this man . . .

She moved her body gingerly. 'Oh, don't worry,' he said, glancing down at her, his hands on his hips, 'I don't think you've done yourself any damage, apart from a very sore behind——' he permitted himself a faint smile '—and even that dainty little posterior isn't as damaged as your pride. That's what really took a tumble, isn't it, but if you will show off, well——' He shrugged.

It was true. She *had* been showing off dreadfully, but she knew that already, she thought, and didn't need *him* to point it out to her. Very slowly, as though her bruised body were made of exquisitely fine old porcelain, she made a move to stand up, biting her lip hard so that no groan should escape her. But then a pair of strong hands were under her arms and his fingers brushed fleetingly across her breasts.

'Upsadaisy,' a soft, mocking voice said in her ear and she found herself being dumped unceremoniously on her feet. She turned her head away and took hold of Pepe's bridle, mechanically stroking his nose while all the time she was conscious only of her skin, still burning from the light, careless touch of his fingers.

She shot a look down at him but his head was bent and she could only see the thick, shaggy thatch of dark hair, brushed with a faint streak of grey at the temple. She leaned her head against Pepe's warm neck, watching the lean brown fingers as they probed the horse's leg. His hands were so delicate, yet so suggestive of strength . . . What would it be like to feel those hands moving over her body, caressing, exploring ...? Horrified, Catherine caught herself up as a scalding blush burst all over her face, and in that same instant, as though sensing her turmoil, he glanced up directly at her. Something intangible quickened in his remote grey eyes and hers locked with his until he turned back to his task and Catherine, her heart pounding painfully against her ribs, stared out to sea over the arch of Pepe's neck.

As soon as he had knotted the last piece of improvised bandage in place, she loosed the bridle and turned away. The heat had burned itself out of her body and she now felt chilled in spite of the power of the sun. Her riding-hat had fallen off and as she bent to retrieve it a sudden wave of nausea swept over her and she clapped her hand to her mouth.

Next moment, he had caught her up in his arms and was striding up the beach while she could only lean her head against his bare chest as her stomach churned alarmingly. She opened her eyes to find him staring down at her, their faces only a few inches apart, but even as she began to feel faintly self-conscious under the searching scrutiny of those opaque eyes her expression changed to one of alarm.

'Help! Put me down—I'm going to be sick!' she wailed, and she was. As she alternately groaned and retched, the humiliation she was feeling was far, far worse than any physical discomfort. She flapped an arm at him.

'Go away—*please* go away.'

But he stayed by her, holding her shoulders, until she felt that she would surely die of shame. When at last, gasping, she leaned her clammy forehead against her knee, he said, in a voice which was surprisingly gentle, 'Come on,' and he lifted her up again, to deposit her in a dilapidated beach chair outside his hut.

'I won't take you inside—it might offend your delicate sensibilities,' he said, with something of his former brusqueness, then went inside for a moment, returning with a sweater which he dropped in her lap. 'Put it on—you're shivering.'

The sweater was enormous and very shabby, but as she pulled it over her head the rough scratchiness of the wool was strangely comforting against her skin. He left her for a few minutes, then came back with a hunk of bread and a mug of steaming tea.

'Condensed milk, I'm afraid, but it'll settle your stomach.'

Catherine detested sweet tea but she drank it in subdued silence and then, suddenly very hungry, demolished the bread. He'd been right; by the time she'd finished the bread and was brushing the crumbs from his sweater she felt fine again.

'Thank you—and I'm sorry I was so stupid, being sick all over the place.' She gave him a half-smile but he did not respond so she went on, 'It must have been the after-effects of the flight yesterday, and I didn't feel like any lunch.'

'More likely those rum punches Nick Alvarez was plying you with last night.'

'One—please.' Her voice was very cold now. 'I had *one* rum punch.'

'Well, all right—even one of those lethal concoctions is too much for a child like you.'

Catherine's gasp of indignation was real, not affected, and she jumped to her feet. 'I'm—nearly twenty-two. I'm *not* a child!'

'Yes—I can see that.' His hard, unyielding eyes flicked deliberately up and down the curves of her body, so that she felt a shiver of apprehension and that same instinctive urge to hug herself protectively while his glance first enwrapped her, as though physically drawing her to him for an instant, then just as casually dropped her.

Catherine stared at the sand. Never in her life, she

thought almost with bewilderment, had she met anyone
remotely like this cool, withdrawn stranger. She glanced
up to where he was leaning against the trunk of a palm-
tree, watching her idly from beneath the tilted brim of his
hat. His very nonchalance inflamed her.

'Oh, and by the way,' she spoke slowly, with the frigid
politeness she only ever used when she was trying to
control deep anger, 'Nick Alvarez happens to be a very
old, very *dear*, friend of mine. He at least works for his
living, and as for you trying to tell me what I should or
should not drink——' her face flushed '—no one,
particularly not a man who goes out of his way to be as—
as unbearable as he can be whenever we meet is going to
tell me what to do, so just mind your own business in
future, will you.'

The smile that flickered across his lips infuriated her
even more and she went on, the words tumbling from
her, 'Everybody always seems to think I need to be told
how to behave! I may have to take it from Uncle Bob—
but I'm not taking it from you!'

She tore off the sweater and went to stand up but in an
instant he had uncoiled himself from the tree to drop on
the sand beside her, a detaining hand across her knees.

'Uncle Bob? You don't mean Bob Latham?'

'Yes. At least, he isn't really my uncle, but I've
always——'

'So you're Catherine Hartley.' He was looking at her in
a way she did not quite like. 'I suppose I should have
known.'

'Known what?' she snapped, responding to the
sardonic note in his voice.

'Oh, that you're the English girl I've heard so much
about. Well, I suppose she couldn't be anyone else but
you, could she?'

The studied insolence in his tone stung her to retaliate.
'And you must be that worthless, idle layabout my uncle
was telling me about last night. From the description, I

did just wonder if it could possibly be you.'

He laughed mirthlessly. 'Yes—I've had occasion to cross swords with Bob Latham. At least, he's tried to cross swords with me a few times lately—he really will have to watch his blood pressure. The funny thing is, there doesn't seem anything special about this particular beach, and yet he will keep trying to persuade me to move out. It's all very puzzling to a simple-minded layabout like me.'

Catherine shot him a sideways glance from under her lashes and caught, surely, in his wintry grey eyes a glint of secret amusement. Her pulses raced with alarm. Was it possible? Did he know about the sale? No, of course not—Uncle Bob had been so insistent on total secrecy. He was just, for his own private pleasure, being as bloody-minded as he knew how. Nevertheless, the warning-bell still jangled—she would have to tread very carefully, for she also knew, with sudden clarity, that her uncle had been utterly wrong in his assessment of this man. Far from being an indolent drifter, he could be a dangerous, ruthless adversary if he so chose. But she would fight back just as ruthlessly, she told herself fiercely.

She had become so engrossed in her own thoughts that she almost didn't hear him. 'Ah, yes—of course,' his voice was reflective, 'I remember now. You're the bloated plutocrat who owns this little bit of real estate.'

'Real estate!' Catherine was pleased with the scorn she managed to inject into the words. 'That's a little grandiose for this piece of scrub! But yes, I do own a couple of plots.'

'Oh, you're too modest.' His strong white teeth gleamed for a moment against his tanned skin, making Catherine think of the predatory smile of a wolf in the fairy stories. 'Quite a lot, from what I hear . . . Well, well, so you're my landlady.' He looked at her consideringly.' 'We'll have to come to some little—arrangement over the rent. The trouble is, I'm perennially short of the ready. Let's see now ... . If only it were the other way round, and I were *your* landlord, I'm sure we could agree on how you could—er, pay your rent.'

Catherine felt the burning colour leap to her cheeks at the mockery patent in his voice and it was too much for her self-control. She jerked back, away from his detaining arm, and when he effortlessly tightened his grip on her she seized his arm and dug her nails hard into the flesh. He winced and withdrew his arm sharply, rubbing it.

'Cat by name—and obviously cat by nature,' he remarked. 'And I was only going to say I'd be delighted to share my fold-up bed with you, if you were my tenant.'

She sprang to her feet and glared angrily down at him, her hands bunched into fists. 'Just get off my land, will you?'

He smiled lazily up at her. 'Why?'

'Just do it. I don't care where you go—I want you off my land—and soon, or I'll, I'll——'

'Or you'll what? Don't forget I have the law on my side. Oh yes, other people besides your precious uncle can read law books, you know. I'm afraid you're stuck with me, honey.'

Catherine was panting for breath. 'Oh, you—you—I tell you, I'll get rid of you!'

'Now, now don't lose your rag.' He shook his head reprovingly and reached over to brush a finger lightly up her leg so that she jumped as though she'd been stung. 'You capitalists are all the same—greedy, money-grubbing. I'm not harming your beach. On the contrary, it's a good deal tidier than when I arrived—I cleared up and buried a large patch of oil which was a danger to wild life, I've removed piles of rubbish brought in by winter storms and I use the driftwood for my fire—apart, that is, from what I sell to your aunt at an exorbitant price. So you see, Cat, I'm quite a useful fellow to have around really, as I'm sure you'll come to realise in time. Just regard me as your gamekeeper, or bailiff or whatever—don't be selfish, share your beach with me.'

Catherine glowered down at him, all discretion now flung to the four winds. 'Oh, God, spare me, please. I can't stand this pose of half-baked "all one big brotherhood, share and share alike"—and it *is* a pose, I know. Don't ask me how, but I do know,' she went on defiantly, as he leapt to his feet and stood over her threateningly. 'You're no more a hippy, flowers-in-your-hair type, than—than I am. It just suits you to pretend you are, on the good old-fashioned principle of "they've got land and wealth and they don't deserve it, so I'll take it off them because I do."'

She glared up at him then, seeing his expression, took a step backwards out of reach, but she was too late. With a violent movement he seized her by the shoulders and pulled her towards him.

'That's enough, Cat—you talk too much!' His voice was rasping. 'And now,' his grip tightened on her even more as she struggled ineffectually to free herself, '—and now, I'll pay my first week's rent.'

She twisted her head away sharply but he gripped her by a handful of her long hair and, as tears of pain sprang to her eyes, wrenched her face back towards his and his lips came down on hers. There was no softness in his touch—just a barely smothered hostility. His mouth against hers, through the tang of saltiness, was hard and demanding and he thrust his tongue between her teeth into the softness of her mouth with a savage intensity which shocked her.

Catherine, locked against him, one hand gripping fiercely on her shoulder, the other, the fingers splayed through her hair, fought frantically to break free. But then slowly, infinitely slowly, his kiss became gentler, his tongue probing delicately, intimately, on and on, until she leaned against him and yielded herself to him, her heart thundering in her ears. Her senses were avid for the touch of his silken-smooth yet hard body against hers, and when he began to trail his lips softly over her cheeks, under her ears and down the throbbing pulse in her throat, she closed her eyes with a tiny moan of pleasure.

When he released her, quite suddenly, dizzy and breathless, she was forced to steady herself against him for a moment. Then she heard a mocking voice in her ear. 'That's something on account for next week's rent as well.'

Catherine drew a deep breath and, silently raging at herself for betraying such weakness, brushed the last bits of sand off her shorts as nonchalantly as she could manage and then, ignoring him, began to walk away down the beach. She thought at first he wasn't going to follow her, but he caught her up as she reached Pepe, still standing quietly where they had left him. She shook the tumbling curtain of hair round her face, unwilling for him to see her flushed cheeks and swollen mouth, and began to untie the bridle with unsteady hands.

'And what do you think you're doing?'

'I'm going home.'

'Not on Pepe, you're not. You'll have to walk.'

He took the bridle but she snatched it away from him. 'There's nothing wrong with him. Look at him—he isn't even limping.'

In fact, she had had no intention of riding Pepe, and had been resigning herself to the long walk back along the beach to the stables, but as usual he had raised her hackles. She took a firm grip of the bridle, feeling slightly foolish and not at all sure what she was going to do, but his hands fastened on hers like vices and, looking down, she could only watch as he prised open her fingers one by one.

'You are *not* riding him, and that's final. Just get that into your stupid little head, will you?' He peeled away the last finger and pulled her clear of the horse.

'Just who do you think you are!' Catherine blazed at him. 'You may have been able to make me kiss you——'

'*Make* you? Honey, you were ready and willing. I should think you're more than a match for Alvarez—quite a handful, in fact.'

'Oh, you—you go to hell!'

Quite beside herself now, she launched a hefty kick at him. Although she was only wearing trainers, a great deal of venom went into the kick and she caught him on the ankle. He flinched and looked down at her, his face flushed under the deep tan.

'You know, you really are a little she-cat,' he said, obviously keeping his voice level with an effort. 'First you claw my arm, then you spit fire at me, now you savage my ankle. It's time someone taught you a lesson, and it may as well be me.'

Catherine, suddenly frightened, turned to run, but he was on her before she had gone a dozen steps. He snatched her up and, ignoring her struggles and her fists beating futilely against his chest, he carried her down the beach, splashed out through the shallows and flung her into the water. It was not at all deep but she was helpless to save herself and fell heavily, going right under. She came up, coughing and gasping, water showering from her, to see him standing on the edge, watching her, a faint smile on his face. She knew that she must look a sight, and at any other time her sense of humour would have asserted itself, but at that smile she stuck her nose in the air and, coughing and breathless, began to wade towards the shore, ignoring him totally.

He came over to her as she took hold of Pepe's bridle.

'I told you, you're not to ride him.'

'I am *not* riding him,' she said through her teeth, not looking at him. 'I'm going to lead him along the beach.'

'Oh, leave him with me. I told Henry I'd give him a hand grooming them all tonight.' Then, as he saw her expression, he added, 'Well, even a beach-bum must eat, you know. So I'll take him back with me.'

Impatiently, she dropped the bridle and began to squelch off up the beach, shaking the wet strands of hair back over her shoulders, but he caught her up again.

'Where are you off to now?'

'If you must know, I'm going out to the road to hitch a lift into town. Not that I really care where I go,' she added, 'just so long as it's away from here.'

'Is that wise—at least, until you've dried off a bit?'

'What do you mean?'

'W—e—ll.' He smiled provocatively, allowing his eyes to wander over her body again. Catherine glanced down, then realised only too clearly what he meant. That afternoon, for her ride, she had dressed for coolness—cotton shorts and a loose blue cotton top, and no bra. Now—she swallowed hard—her shorts were bad enough. The outline of her white pants was showing clearly through the wet pink cotton. But her blouse, still dripping sea water, was moulded to her body like a second skin, revealing the high rounded curves of her breasts and the firmness of her nipples as though she were naked. For one terrifed moment she thought he was going to seize her again and she instinctively stepped back, but he merely laughed and, with a sweep of his hand, made an ironic gesture of dismissal.

Her face scarlet, she turned away. But he was right—she couldn't possibly thumb a lift. No, she would have to walk every inch of the hot way trusting that her clothes would have dried on her before she reached town. She climbed stiffly over the groyne and dropped on to the soft, shifting sand on the other side. Her wet, sandy trainers were beginning to rub against her feet so, grimly, she kicked them off and began to walk barefoot, the sand burning under the soles of her feet.

'Hey, Cat, you've forgotten this.'

She turned as something landed with a soft thud just behind her. It was her riding-hat and as she snatched it up she heard his voice.

'Enjoy your walk, Cat.' And his hateful laugh pursued her as she made her way along the shore.

CHAPTER FOUR

'LETTER for you.'

Lucilla dropped the blue airmail form into Catherine's lap and flopped down beside her on the veranda, fanning herself with her sun-hat. Catherine slit the letter open with her thumb-nail and skimmed through the contents.

'It's from Maggie—my flat-mate in London.'

'She's well, I hope?'

'Oh, yes, fine.' Catherine spoke absently. 'She's had an offer to share a larger flat and wants to know if I'm going back.' She shot Aunt Lu a glance.

'But surely there's no question of that?'

'Well——' Catherine hesitated, then plunged on. 'I haven't had a chance to talk to you about it before, but— I'd almost decided not to go back anyway. I—I only got a one-way air ticket. And now I *have* decided—I'm staying in St Hilaire, for good this time.' She smiled rather tremulously across at the other woman. 'Aren't you pleased? I thought you would be.'

Lucilla took her hand. 'It's not that I'm not pleased, honey,' she said slowly, 'and you know Robert will be over the moon. It's just—is it best for you? I ask myself, what would your Daddy want—he was so proud of that brain of yours, and I know he'd have wanted you to have a *real* career, even if it meant your staying in England.'

'But Dad and Mum aren't here, and everything's different.' Her lip trembled slightly, but she went on, 'I have to make a life for myself now. I was so lonely in London away from the island, and it was always so cold——' she shivered reminiscently '—and, Aunt Lu, this is my home—*this* is where I want to be.'

Lucilla patted her hand. 'All right, honey, if that's

46

what you want. And you know we'll love having you back.'

'What I thought was, you were saying the other night how you'll find it difficult to run Cinnamon House single-handed when it's all systems go—well, I could work for you. I can type, and I'm quite good at organising. I could be your Girl Friday—meet the guests at the airport, that sort of thing.'

'But when Coral Strand is sold, you won't have to work—you'll be an heiress,' her aunt said teasingly.

'Oh, I'm not letting myself count *those* chickens until they're all sitting on the perch. And anyway, did Uncle Bob tell you my idea—about equipping a nursery-cum-guest-room at the hospital, so that mothers could stay with their sick children and when they're convalescing? Do you remember, that was always one of Mum's pet schemes?'

'Well, yes, he did just mention it.' Lucilla pulled a face and Catherine grinned at her, remembering how he had groaned with horror, and said she must be mad and as soft-centred as her parents.

'It's no use him going on, Aunt Lu,' she said firmly. '*If* I get the money, well, I'm determined to spend some of it in that way as a sort of thank you for all the happy years we had here. And, anyway, I'll still have plenty left, I'm sure.'

'You know, honey, your Mum and Dad are a hard act to follow, but you're doing pretty well. They'd be very proud of you.' Lucilla smiled lovingly at the girl. 'As for working for me—well, I'd love to have you. I'll certainly need some help. The builders will be starting work on the old stables any day, converting half into luxury studio apartments and the rest into a boutique.'

'You're having a boutique?' Catherine looked at her in amazement.

Her aunt laughed. 'Yes—and no matter what Robert says, I'm certain it's a good idea. There are the Indian

bazaars in town, and there's Mrs Munoz—not a silk dress
under three hundred dollars—and nothing in between.
There's plenty of room for the Cinnamon Boutique, I'm
sure.'

'Well, I think it's a great idea—and I'll be glad to help
you whenever you need me. So no more arguing——' she
took Lucilla's hands in hers and shook them slightly
'—and tell Uncle Bob my mind's quite made up over the
money.'

'All right, Cathy, and if you really want to work for me,
you can start tomorrow. The first bungalow is just about
ready, so you can help me with the finishing touches—
putting up pictures and so on. And Mandy, one of the
girls who's doing my batik, rang to say she'd be calling
over in the afternoon with a pair of curtains that she's
finished, but I've just remembered I have a dental
appointment——'

'—so you'd like me to be there when she comes? That's
fine.'

'If you're certain you've nothing more exciting to do.'

Catherine laughed. 'Hardly. On the flight I was
looking forward to a non-stop round of beach picnics,
barbecue parties—but everyone's too busy, or off the
island. So——' she spread her hands in a gesture of
resignation '—you'll be doing me a favour. I wasn't
exactly looking forward to yet another solitary day on the
beach!'

Catherine yawned and stretched her limbs luxuriously,
then clutched the sides of Uncle Bob's hammock as the
two sturdy palms between which it was slung creaked
gently. After a hot morning's work in the bungalow she
was thoroughly enjoying her siesta. She stretched again
like a cat, then wriggled her shoulders as she felt the
thong side straps of her bikini dig into her flesh. She had
rediscovered her old black bikini in the linen press some
days before, but after trying it on had not dared wear it

on the beach, although it was ideal in the total privacy of the garden of Cinnamon House. She loosened the clasp and, with a faint groan of relief, eased herself out of it slightly, thinking ruefully, Oh, those apple pies, those plum crumbles!

She lay back and closed her eyes, fanning herself with her book, for even up here on the hillside looking down on Port Charlotte, hazed by the afternoon sun, the air was stifling, without even the faintest whisper of a cooling wind.

Then she opened the book again. It had seemed a positive pleasure to be able to read without the pressure and tensions of looming exams, but after a few minutes, utterly defeated by the heat, she laid the volume face down on her stomach and, reaching down into the fruit bowl on the grass beside her, picked out a large mango. The skin was warm under her fingers as she peeled it, then she dug her teeth into the succulent golden flesh. Bliss, pure bliss, she thought. The palms rustled softly overhead . . . an insect cricked plaintively in the bushes . . . a car engine laboured up the steep road . . . the hammock swayed in rhythm with her gentle breathing. A trickle of juice ran slowly down her arm and she scooped it up sensuously with her tongue.

She had not heard the soft footfalls on the carefully tended lawn, and the first warning she had was when a dark shape loomed between her and the dazzling sunlight. She screwed up her eyes uncertainly, for a moment quite unable to put a name to the outline, but then she sucked in her breath in a gasp as she recognised her visitor. Instinctively, she jerked upright, the hammock swung violently and she shot out of it, to sprawl in an untidy heap on the grass, looking up at him.

Luke Devinish made no effort to help her but he gave a low chuckle and his lips curved in open amusement at her discomfiture. Catherine scrambled to her feet, rubbing her elbow angrily.

'What do *you* want?' she demanded.

He raised his eyebrows. 'Before you start being your usual charming self, you really should haul yourself back into that bikini.'

His eyes wandered down her body and Catherine, following his glance, realised that with the clasp already loosened the tumble had done the rest and most of her breasts, including the dusky rose aureoles of her nipples, were exposed to his mocking gaze. Scarlet-faced and with her skin crawling under the almost physical assault of his eyes, she snatched up the matching black towelling top and dragged it down fiercely over her head and shoulders. He tilted back his straw hat and watched her, his grey eyes narrowed with an ironic amusement which she tried to ignore.

'What do you want?' she repeated stonily and had the dubious satisfaction of seeing his smile fade, leaving his lips a thin line.

'I went to the house but there was no one about,' he answered shortly.

'So you invited yourself round here.' Catherine's voice was cool and she was eyeing him across the hammock, as a tennis player might watch his adversary across the net in a vital match.

'Don't be more stupid than you have to be. I came to see your aunt—is she about?'

'No—and she won't be back for several hours, so there's no point in your waiting.'

She went to walk past him but he caught her arm and roughly swung her towards him. Her eyes jerked up to his face and saw such pent-up anger flaring in his that, instinctively, she flinched away from him, afraid that he would strike her.

'Tell me, Cattie,' his voice grated in her ear, 'hasn't anyone ever put you over their knee and given you a damned good hiding? It's what you need, desperately.'

His fingers tightened on her arm and he shook her,

then just as suddenly as he had caught her he loosened his grip. He thrust her away from him, as though afraid of his own reaction, so that she sank into a chair, staring up at him in shocked astonishment.

For a few moments she was breathing so rapidly that she was unable to speak but then she panted, 'I've told you, my aunt isn't here.' Then, remembering that, technically at least, she was now working for Aunt Lu, she added, 'I'll tell her you called, Mr Devinish. Good afternoon.'

But instead of taking her not-so-subtle hint, he hooked his foot round a patio chair and dropped into it beside her. Catherine's throat was suddenly dry. She told herself stoutly that this was *her* territory—or, at least, Uncle Bob's—and yet again he was the intruder. But in that case, the intruder should be apologetic, ill at ease— cringing even—while instead, she thought with a surge of mingled anger and fear, his cool grey eyes were watching her with an expression that warned her that, her territory or not, he would not leave until he was good and ready. Her fingers bunched in her lap. It was utterly ridiculous. Every time they met he was in the weaker position, yet within thirty seconds, by the sheer brute force of his personality, he was imposing his will on her.

She came out of her reverie to realise that he was speaking and that his voice was marginally warmer. 'I was merely going to say, before you yet again pinned on your sheriff's badge and tried to run me out of town, that I thought I might have inadvertently strayed into the Perfumed Garden. It's all here—exotic flowers, hum- ming birds, and a beautiful nymph, lying in a hammock and eating a mango in the sexiest possible way—I often think the mango must have been the original forbidden fruit, don't you?'

Catherine looked up to find his eyes on her face again. There was secret amusement in his gaze, amusement at a private joke which, she was quite sure, she would not wish to share.

'By the way, I nearly forgot.' There was a subtle provocation in his voice. 'Did you enjoy your walk last week?'

At the memory of their last humiliating encounter and of her broiling trek along the beach her lips tightened, and she ignored his question. 'I hope you've come to tell us that you're getting off our land.'

'Oh dear, must you bring that unpleasant topic up, Cattie, just when we're getting on so well?' He gave a dramatic sigh, but the look he shot her conveyed that clear warning again.

Catherine fought to control herself. She suddenly had the feeling that they were playing some strange cat-and-mouse game, she and Luke—for, with a sinking heart, she knew that this was between them. Uncle Bob might just as well not exist, he had no real part to play. And she also knew which of them had devised the rules of this game and who had been cast as the mouse.

'We are not getting on well,' she said woodenly, 'and I would like you, please, to leave my land—that is as soon as it is convenient to you.'

'But I'm afraid it isn't convenient.'

Catherine decided to be businesslike. 'Look, in case you think Mr Latham wasn't serious about the offer of money, I've discussed the matter of your continued occupation of Coral Strand with him several times——' in fact, she had mentioned it once and Uncle Bob had fallen into such a rage that she, alarmed for his blood pressure, had changed the conversation '—and I have authorised him, on my behalf, to offer you more—in fact, a remarkably generous amount, that will enable you to leave St Hilaire and travel to another——'

'Get it into your cotton-wool head,' the savagery in his voice shocked her, 'that contrary to what you and your precious uncle may believe, not every man has his price. I am not interested in your filthy money. My God, I thought Latham was bad enough——'

'You keep Uncle Bob out of this!' Catherine flared. 'You know nothing—nothing about him.'

'Oh, don't I just? Tell me this then, what am I supposed to think of a man who's prepared to let a beautiful little beach like Coral Strand fall into the hands of Brannan International?'

'Brannan International!' Catherine gasped involuntarily, then tried desperately to disguise the tremendous shock that his words had created in her. 'W-what on earth are you talking about?'

'Oh, come off it. Don't try to play the innocent with me, sweetie. You know damned well what I'm talking about—you and Latham hatching up that cosy little arrangement with Brannan.' He laughed mirthlessly. 'You surely didn't think a deal like that could be kept under wraps for long in a place like St Hilaire, did you?'

No, Catherine thought ruefully, of course not. Certainly not in Port Charlotte, where the hotline of rumour and gossip was permanently alive and buzzing. No, in spite of Uncle Bob's best efforts, the news had somehow seeped out and had even reached as far as this newcomer, this stranger. The Lord Nelson—of course, that was where he'd picked up this particular juicy piece of information. And—she could barely suppress a shudder of apprehension—what use did he intend to make of it? She looked up into his unsmiling face. This surely must make it all the more difficult to persuade him to move from Coral Strand of his own free will. At the very least, his vindictive pleasure would have been increased tenfold by her obvious dismay at this revelation of his knowledge of the proposed sale.

'If you really are so set on selling,' he went on, in a quieter tone, 'why must it be to Brannan, of all companies?'

He looked at her questioningly and Catherine bridled.

'What business is it of yours? Who are you to presume to come here and tell me what to do and what not to do? You don't even belong here. You're an outsider!'

'You don't seem to have any scruples about selling to a group of outsiders,' he retorted. 'And anyway, I've been here long enough to see that Coral Strand is the most beautiful, unspoilt beach on the whole island, and you two are willing and eager to sell it to a soulless, rapacious company like Brannan. Surely you must know that as far as Brannan are concerned, beauty is simply a saleable commodity, something to be seized, possessed, ravished!'

Catherine stared at him wide-eyed, almost stunned by the pent-up savagery in his voice. Surely there was something more behind his words than anger at the sale of one small beach, however beautiful it might be? Yes— there was some deep personal antagonism here, which she had glimpsed for one frightening moment. Why did he hate Brannan so much—for it surely was a deep hatred that lay behind his outburst? And she saw now that there was something so coldly implacable in this man that it was as though he was bent on exacting some private, personal retribution from Brannan.

'And just who the hell do you think you are,' she burst out, 'with your holier-than-thou ideas about beauty? Don't you preach your half-baked morality at me, as though I'm some kind of vandal. Whatever agreement we may sign, I'm going to ensure that there are clauses protecting Coral Strand, to make sure it stays as unspoilt as it can be. They aren't going to be allowed to put up some horrible, anonymous monstrosity.'

Luke's laugh was almost a sneer. 'You're either even more devious or more naïve than I took you for. Don't you understand that once Brannan get their greedy hands on that piece of land they aren't going to let a few pious words on a scrap of paper come between them and their profits.'

'No,' said Catherine firmly, recalling Uncle Bob's words. 'You're wrong there. I happen to know that Mr Brannan himself is a stickler for the law. Anything he puts his name to, he'll abide by.'

'Old man Brannan? Yes, you may be right. But he's no longer the driving force. There's a new generation coming up who don't exactly share his scruples, for whom a contract, any contract, is just something to be manipulated to their own advantage.'

This wasn't what Uncle Bob had said. And yet Luke seemed so confident of his facts—or was it just bluster, another move in his war to outmanoeuvre *her*? Surely Uncle Bob was right—after all, he'd been dealing with them face to face. Still, it would be wiser not to argue the point at this stage—perhaps she should even make Luke think that she at least half accepted what he had said. She might even be able to turn it to her advantage.

'If you *are* right,' she said, forcing herself to meet his level gaze, 'you'd better watch out. As soon as we've sold to Brannan, they'll move the bulldozers in and make short shrift of one squatter, however certain of his legal rights he may be.'

'But you're forgetting one tiny thing, honey. As long as I choose to stay, the land isn't yours to sell.'

'Oh yes, thanks to some legal technicality.' Catherine was really angry now. 'But by every moral law, Coral Strand is ours and you know it!'

'Maybe. But there's not a damned thing you can do about it, is there?'

His eyes were mocking yet appraising her, as if to see just how far she could be driven, and Catherine sat back in her chair, biting her lip and thinking furiously. She glanced at him under her lashes as he lounged back, completely at his ease but clearly all set to resume the combat if necessary. She looked away from him, for the moment totally baffled. There was absolutely no point in prolonging this. The man beside her was clearly in no

mood to listen to reason, and she certainly wasn't going
to demean herself by begging him to leave Coral Strand.
She could guess all too well what such a plea would
evoke. On the other hand, he was clearly in no hurry to
go, and she was not going to humiliate herself further by
beating an ignominious retreat.

They sat without speaking for some moments, but
finally the silence unnerved her and she felt she had to
speak, if only to bring the atmosphere down to a safer,
less explosive level.

'You said you came to see my aunt.' Her voice was
coldly formal. 'I'm working for her now so perhaps I can
deal with it, then there'll be no need for you to wait.'

'I've brought her this.'

He gestured casually and Catherine saw that on the
grass beside him was an enormous conch shell, the
largest she had ever seen. Spontaneously, she moved
forward and sank to her knees beside it then gently
picked it up, feeling its heavy weight on her hands.

'It's beautiful,' she cried, 'really beautiful!' Then she
remembered, with a sick feeling, the cruel way in which
the living creatures inside the shells were removed, and
she looked up at him.

'Did you——?'

'Did I prepare the shell myself? No, I got it from a guy
along the coast. So don't worry,' he added, with a hint of
irony, 'these aren't butcher's hands.'

But they could be, she thought, with a constriction of
the throat. Those fingers could be precise, cruel, ruthless . . . She turned her attention back to the shell, faintly
cream on the outside, shading through to pale grey down
the lovely spiral of whorls to its white tip. The delicate,
translucent fluting round its edge was like a ruff of
starched lace, then the colour deepened gradually to a
moss-rose pink, so that when she held it up to the light
the shade glowed through the entire shell. Soothed by its
beauty, she began gently stroking its glossy, pink curve.

Intent upon the shell, she had momentarily forgotten Luke but then she became aware that he was kneeling beside her and was lightly running one finger up her arm, his hand in perfect time with her fingers as they stroked the shell. The pressure was so light that Catherine felt the little golden hairs on her skin prickle under his touch and the parallel rhythms of their fingers seemed to set up matching echoes in her brain. For a moment she allowed a strange quiver of pleasure to run through her but then, dry-mouthed, she shivered and drew back. Now very conscious of the man beside her, so close that she caught the faint tang of his body, she panicked.

Her heart beating irregularly, she set down the conch clumsily, so that it rolled over, then she sat back and tried to gather her composure. She would retreat to the sanctuary of the house—she couldn't stay here any longer. Her fingers groped blindly for her book but she was too late and his hand had closed on it, withdrawing it from her grasp.

As Catherine held out her hand he glanced down at the cover then back to her, his eyebrows raised sardonically. '*The Love Poems of John Donne*—hmmm, strong meat for a hot afternoon.'

Catherine, feeling the colour race into her cheeks, said quietly, 'Give me my book, please.'

She avoided his eyes and went to stand up, but lazily he hooked one foot round the front leg of her chair and jerked it towards him.

'Yes,' he went on reflectively, 'John Donne, a nearly naked girl in a hammock, eating tropical fruit—it all adds up to something pretty sexy.'

Without the least haste, he ran one tanned finger softly up her arm again as Catherine watched, mesmerised, her whole body transfixed. This is madness, she thought, I must get away from him. Yet even as she thought this, she felt herself sway closer to the pressure of that finger, her eyes half closing.

Then, without opening the book, he murmured, as though to himself, '"I wonder, by my troth, what thou and I did, till we loved?"'

Her eyes opened wide in unfeigned astonishment and she drew back her arm as though he had burned it. How, she asked herself, how, by some dreadful unerring instinct, had he picked on her favourite poem? The surprise was succeeded immediately by anger. Why was this man never content to accept the role she wanted for him? It would be so much easier to dismiss him from her mind as an idle, freewheeling waster, but yet again she had the overwhelming sensation that there was very much more to him than this. And why must he constantly force himself on her notice, when she wanted nothing more than to forget his very existence? Once more he was thrusting his way into her life, this time not on to the physical territory of her beach but into the intensely private world of her beloved poetry.

But on no account must he be allowed to guess the depth of her feelings. 'D-do you like the metaphysical poets?' she asked, striving to appear casual.

'It depends. I like Donne; he matches so exactly my moods—all of them. Anyway, what's so surprising? You really must get it out of your little head that all layabouts are completely illiterate. Some of us can count up to ten on our fingers, you know, and I learned to read—oh, a couple of years ago now. No, some of us are quite interesting guys, although I know it would disturb your equilibrium to have to admit it.'

As Catherine fought to hide her mingled annoyance and chagrin at this latest display of his apparently uncanny way of reading her mind, he went on reflectively, 'But mind you, Cattie, *reading* about love is only half of it, isn't it? That is, unless you're just using it as a substitute for the real thing.'

'Wh-what do you mean, a substitute?' Even to her own ears, her voice was croaky.

'Well, you can't get hurt that way, can you?' She felt his finger brush lightly up her arm again, leaving her skin tingling. 'If you do no more than lie here sedately, reading about it, there's no chance of you being scorched, burned—consumed by love, is there?'

His voice was soft yet it had a subtle, seductive quality about it that was weaving a sensual spell around her, relentlessly drawing her to him. 'I wonder if you would want to risk that, Cattie. I rather think you might—at least, with the right man.'

Catherine sat forward rigidly in her chair. She wanted to argue, to protest, to free herself from his spell but his hypnotic voice in her ear, the insidious movement of his finger, held her prisoner. Her whole body quivered involunatrily as she suddenly felt his hand slide from her arm, under her beach-top, to rest against the small of her back.

'"License my roving hands, and let them go
Before, behind, between, above, below . . ."'

His voice was a gentle murmur and his thumb was slowly, lazily, caressing her spine. His touch, though light and unhurried, was setting off a train of tiny electric sparks beneath her warm skin until Catherine, the pulses beating in her head, shivered with delicious apprehension. Her reason told her that she must at all costs break free of this new enchantment, but her body was gripped by a warm languor which flowed through her like quicksilver, willing her to surrender entirely to the power of his voice.

'"Oh, my America—my new-found land,
My mine of precious stones, my empiry,
How blest I am in thus discovering thee . . ."'

Luke slid his hand to the base of her spine and rested there, his fingers splayed against the softness of her flesh. Catherine's breathing deepened and she felt as though she were drowning in a sea of sensuous delight. Around her, the garden was holding its breath. Wafts of heady perfume came to her from a sweetly scented shrub and through her almost closed eyes she saw a tiny jewelled humming-bird hang in the air, to thrust itself time and again into the flared trumpet of a crimson hibiscus flower.

'On the other hand, perhaps he was nearer the mark with "And swear, No where, lives a woman true and fair." I think that has more of the ring of truth, don't you?'

Luke's voice was suddenly harsh. Her mind still drowsy under the sensuous spell, Catherine scarcely realised that his hand had gone from her body and she opened her eyes in utter bewilderment to meet his gaze, bleak and cold as some half-frozen Arctic sea, his glance that of the contemptuous, stony-faced stranger she had first encountered on the beach. Completely disorientated by this swift change of mood, and still mesmerised by the spell he had cast, she simply stared at him, unable to speak.

'Well—don't you agree?'

The grating sarcasm in his voice made her wince. 'No—no, I don't,' she stammered at last. 'I don't like it at all—it's so cynical, so cold-hearted.'

He gave a short, mirthless laugh. 'And you don't think, by any chance, that he might have been driven to write that way by some little—tramp!' He spat out the word as though it sickened him and as Catherine sat in stunned silence he went on, 'Surely, all women are whores at heart, aren't they—given half a chance, that is? And you'd be no better than the rest, would you, lady?'

He twisted her towards him, his fingers digging in her flesh, so close that she was forced to look into his eyes— the darker rim around the grey, the intensely black pupils, the sweep of charcoal lashes.

'Would you?' he repeated and gave her head an angry shake. 'Beautiful, wide-apart, innocent eyes—blurring with tears——' Catherine hastily blinked them away

'—eyes a man could drown in. Yet look at you—look at
yourself. You loathe me—a no-good, worthless bum,
that's how you see me, isn't it? But a few soft words, my
hand on your skin—that was all that was needed, wasn't
it?'

He tilted her face, then, with a dismissive gesture,
thrust her away from him. Catherine's whole body was
shaking and there was a bitter, burning taste in her
mouth. She wanted to get up, to run and hide herself, but
when she tried to move her legs had been transformed
into flimsy matchsticks. She turned to him, almost
pleadingly, willing him to take back those dreadful
words, but at the sight of his face, the cruel pleasure at
her bewilderment so clearly written on it, the words she
would have spoken died on her lips.

She saw now, with a dreadful certainty, that all the
time he had been caressing her mind and body he had
been coldly, callously playing with her. It was as if he had
been deliberately seeking to confirm his implacably
cynical view of women and at the same time had been
exacting some dreadful private revenge. He was watching her now, as a heartless, unfeeling boy might watch a
fly impaled on a pin, and she herself was fluttering
feebly, unable even to try to defend herself, for very deep
down inside her, way past the detestation of him, the
shame of herself, she knew that her response had proved
him right and his words had been nothing less than the
truth . . .

'Hi, there! Anyone home?' Catherine, her mind still
reeling, looked round to see a young woman coming up
the path towards them. She gripped the arms of her chair
with sweaty hands, trying to quell the shaking of her
body. Avoiding Luke's eyes, she stumbled to her feet and
stood leaning one hand on the back of the chair for
support. The burning colour which had engulfed her at
his words fled, leaving her slightly giddy, but this new
shock was having an almost anaesthetic effect and now a

cold, numbing paralysis was creeping through her distraught mind, cutting her off from the scene with Luke as though she had been a mere spectator.

By the time the young woman reached them, Catherine was outwardly perfectly composed but she was very pale. Her eyes widened as she took in the newcomer. The girl, hardly older than herself, was superb—tall and as lithely slim as a well honed greyhound, a fact emphasised by the slight sway of her body as she walked and the briefest of white shorts and bikini top.

As she sauntered across the grass towards them, Catherine found that she was gaping in open-mouthed astonishment, and hastily closing her mouth, she took a step forward to greet the apparition. But she need not have bothered. Completely ignoring her, the girl tossed her straw beach-bag down on the grass.

'Luke! Where have you been, man?'

Catherine's jaw dropped open again as Luke levered himself out of his chair and grinned at the newcomer.

'Hi, Mandy. Gorgeous as ever, I see.'

Mandy twined her arms round his neck and dropped nibbling kisses down his cheek, saying, between nips, 'Oh, I've missed you, honey.'

Catherine watched, unable to tear her eyes away and feeling herself insipid, almost lumpish by the side of this gorgeous creature. Over Mandy's shoulder, Luke's eyes met hers in a look of malicious amusement and Catherine, realising that she was still gaping, gave him a freezing stare in return.

Mandy released him at last, and ruffling her shining black curls in a thoroughly provocative gesture—or so Catherine thought sourly to herself—said, 'Darling, won't you introduce me to your little friend?' at the same time giving Catherine a cool sideways look.

Little friend! I don't believe this, Catherine thought. Through stiff lips, she said coldly, 'I'll introduce myself. I'm Catherine Hartley, and you must be——'

'Oh, Lu's niece from England.' Mandy's tone was just polite, yet it managed to be supremely dismissive, stinging Catherine on the raw, still off balance as she was from the episode with Luke.

'Yes, Mrs Latham's niece,' she said, with equally cold formality. 'My aunt is out this afternoon, I'm afraid, but she's asked me to look after any of her *staff* who might call.'

'Tch, tch, Cattie,' Luke broke in, then turning to Mandy he said, 'You'll have to excuse the young lady. She thinks she's a cut above the likes of you and me, honest labourers though we may be.'

'You just keep out of this,' Catherine snapped.

'Now, now.' His voice was reproving and his grey eyes were alight with mockery, which fed Catherine's anger.

She opened her mouth to retort but then, just in time, caught the other girl's black eyes on her, narrow and full of sudden speculation, and closed it, biting her lip while she tried to regain control of herself. It was utterly ridiculous for her to allow herself to be dragged into this three-cornered squabble and anyway, she told herself, it would hardly do for Aunt Lu to return on her first day at work to find that, like a young cuckoo, she had turfed out two of her fellow employees!

So she ignored Luke's provocation and thrust her hands into the pockets of her beach-top, clenching her fists, as she forced herself to say very politely, 'You must have brought the batik Aunt Lu was expecting. If you'd like to leave it, I'll see she gets it as soon as she comes back.'

'Sure,' said Mandy and, reaching into her bag, handed Catherine a package. As she took it, a length of cloth spilled out on to the grass and she bent down and shook out the folds, glad to have something physical to do to distract her from the cross-currents that were surging among the three of them. The background of the material was the softest, palest blue-green, and the abstract swirls of pattern, in shades of cinnamon, chocolate and splashes of black, suggested a cool, submarine scene.

Catherine held a drift of cloth over one hand and looked up at the other girl. 'It's really beautiful. Aunt Lu will love it.'

The girl shrugged but looked slightly mollified. 'It's a job,' she said, and began deftly folding the material.

But even as she did so, Luke slid his arm round her glossy shoulders and Catherine watched fascinated, as a rabbit watches a snake, as his thumb began gently stroking up the side of her neck towards her ear, in a gesture at once familiar and possessive.

Afraid suddenly of what her expression might betray, Catherine lowered her eyes and said, 'I'll ask Aunt Lu to give you a ring then, shall I?'

She picked up the cloth, clutching it hard against her chest in an attempt to calm her unsteady breathing, then, leaving them to follow her, went rapidly down the path, trying to get out of earshot of the low, intimate murmurings.

On the drive in front of the house was—Catherine stared at it, almost unable to believe her eyes—a hot pink, open-top beach buggy. Well, it would just have to be something like that, wouldn't it, she thought with an attempt to regain her former asperity, but it was no use— she only felt deflated, drained. Fighting down the urgent desire to retreat into the house and lock the door, she stood by the buggy, trying not to watch as they strolled up, Luke's arm still round the girl's shoulder, his fingers carelessly brushing against the top of her breast.

Ignoring him, she turned to Mandy and said in her most formal voice, 'Do let me get you a drink. A cold lager—or some iced coffee?'

'No thanks, I'm in a hurry.' Mandy gave her a very brief smile then turned back to Luke. 'Darling—you are going to Nick's party on Friday, aren't you?'

Catherine looked at him across the buggy, her tawny

eyes darkening with horror. She had been looking forward immensely to Nick's birthday party, ever since he had invited her a few days earlier, but now . . .

Luke's eyes locked with hers for an instant, then he said, 'Sure, I'll be there.' Then he went on, that glinting look in his eyes that Catherine so detested, 'What's the matter, Cattie? Nick's a generous guy, doesn't like to feel anyone's left out. Surely you're not shocked that a loafer like me should get an invite?'

'No—it's just——' She stopped abruptly.

'Don't worry—I won't disgrace you, although I'm afraid I shan't be able to manage a black tie. Cattie's a bit concerned,' he said conversationally to Mandy, 'that as her tenant, I may let her down dress-wise.'

Catherine, instantly determined that wild horses would not now drag her to the party at the Lord Nelson, managed a stiff-lipped smile that somehow included both of them and neither, and walked away towards the house.

Behind her, she heard Mandy say, 'I'll give you a lift, honey.' Her voice dropped seductively but was still loud enough for Catherine to hear, 'I'm just longing to see that cute little cabin of yours again.'

As she reached the top of the veranda steps, she glanced quickly over her shoulder, in time to see the buggy surging out of the drive in a cloud of reddish dust and away down the road to town. She leaned her hot cheek against one of the veranda pillars and stood quite still, until the last sound of the car had faded. Her eyes were smarting and she closed them against the late afternoon glare. She felt really low, she thought, her head was thumping and there was a strange, sick feeling in the pit of her stomach. She wanted desperately to get home to Hope's Mill and shut herself away in the haven of her own bedroom to let herself finally burst into tears, but she knew instinctively that this would not ease her wretchedness.

She butted her head against the wooden pillar thinking, Oh God, what *is* wrong with me? Perhaps she was ill. Aunt Lu had said there was a lot of denghi fever about. Yes, that was it—she was going down with denghi. Well, at least that would mean she had an excuse for opting out of Nick's party. The party . . . Luke and Mandy, dancing together . . . The truth, a jagged lightning flash, ran through her. It was not fever—it was jealousy, searing jealousy. She was jealous, jealous of Mandy's easy familiarity with Luke, jealous of her kissing him, and jealous of his hand wandering possessively—no doubt through long acquaintance—over her, as she would be jealous of any girl he touched.

She wanted Luke to look at *her* the way he had looked at Mandy. *She* wanted that easy familiarity; *she* wanted to feel his hands, those strong, slender fingers, on her body again—and this time, not playing with her emotions to satisfy, with malicious, cruel pleasure, his deep dislike of her, but because he wanted to, needed to . . .

Sick with self-disgust, she stared at the veranda rail, as though she would memorise every knot in the polished wood. I can't feel like this, she told herself fiercely, I despise, detest, loathe this man. I can't! A wave of chagrin swept through her and she buried her burning face in her hands. Her skin, where he had touched her, seemed to be scorching hot, almost crawling with heat. She couldn't—dared not—wait for Aunt Lu. She found a notepad in her bag, scribbled a few lines, and left it propped up on the bundle of batik where her aunt couldn't miss it. Fumbling for her keys, she almost ran to the car in her frantic anxiety to escape.

CHAPTER FIVE

CATHERINE switched the shower on full, and gasped as the fine needles of cold water hit her hot skin. She forced herself to stay under for long, uncomfortable minutes, turning her body this way and that in the streaming jets, determined to cleanse herself once and for all of every vestige of the touch of Luke's contaminating hands.

At last, she wrapped herself in a bath robe and sat out on the veranda; she felt as though the water had done its work, leaving her skin alive and tingling clean, all trace of Luke gone. But, she reflected, as she sipped the cup of tea that Mattie had brought her, as for her mind—that was another matter. That too seemed to have been defiled, only more insidiously; soap and water had cleansed her body, but her mind was still sick with self-disgust. Why had she stayed in the garden, knowing, the moment he appeared, that she should make a haughty exit? And not only stayed, but had let him *maul* her, toy with her, for his own malicious pleasure? How foolish she had been allowing a hot afternoon, a few lines of poetry and—yes, she had to admit it—an undoubtedly handsome man, conspire to overcome her defences.

Well, it was not going to happen again—ever. And as for the party—she *was* going. It would hurt Nick, her old friend, if she stayed away and, besides, it would be so foolish. Luke would know why she wasn't there, and that would only add to his sense of triumph over her. She must show him that she did not care. He and Mandy could behave—or, more likely, misbehave—exactly as they wished, but she simply would not allow it to be any concern of hers.

But Luke's knowledge of the Brannan deal, that was a

different matter. Her first instinct was to ring Uncle Bob and warn him, but she decided against this. With any luck, with the court case coming up in just a few days, there was no point in worrying him now, for surely the court would find in their favour and sanction the lawful removal of Luke.

Luke ... Who *was* this man who had come from nowhere and who had set himself up so deliberately, as she now saw, against her—and not just against her? She recalled her sudden conviction that there was some personal vendetta here. It was as if he were waging a one-man crusade, not against multi-national companies in general—she could at least have understood that—but all his venom seemed to be directed against Brannan International.

She allowed herself a faint smile, almost feeling sorry for the company. They just did not know what they were up against! Her assessment of him had been right all along. Here was no idle dreamer, fighting a cock-eyed, idealistic battle that could be crushed by one whiff of hard reality. No, however effectively he had assumed his beach-bum role, there was an intelligence and a drive in Luke which would have taken him to the top in any occupation he chose.

And another thing—how had he known about the obscure legal loophole that had enabled him to fight his single-handed battle so effectively? Had he had a legal training? Many lawyers these days moved into the world of big business ... Yes, that was it. Luke could have worked for Brannan ... been one of their high-flying executives ... Perhaps he had been dismissed, unfairly in his view, of course. Had disagreed perhaps with the methods of the new breed of Brannans he had spoken of so scathingly ... He would have been aware of the Coral Strand negotiations and set out quite coldly to sabotage them. In this way he would gain some sort of personal revenge against Brannan but he was clearly utterly uncaring of who else might get hurt in the process . . .

Catherine came out of her reverie, her resolve strengthened further. If he could be so completely unfeeling towards her, she too would be totally careless of him.

It was, therefore, in order to look her best for Nick—and certainly for no other reason—that Catherine prepared herself for the party with such deliberate care. She rubbed body lotion over herself until her skin gleamed and piled up her shiny brown hair into a huge knot. In spite of the freckles across the bridge of her nose, her skin tanned well and all that was needed was a touch of gloss and a dusting of soft brown eyeshadow to tone down the effect of those tawny eyes. She had bought her dress a few days previously in one of the Indian bazaars; it was a loose smock, in fine cream Indian cotton, with heavy matching cotton lace on the bodice and wrists. She tied the drawstrings tightly, edge to edge, then paused, her fingers still on the strings. With a decisive gesture, she loosened them again, so that the neckline revealed the shadowed curve of her breasts. She regarded her unsmiling reflection, then the thought came unbidden into her mind that it was exactly as though she was preparing for war. At that, she laughed and picked up her bag.

'Cathy, darling, you look gorgeous—good enough to eat!' Nick, his voice raised almost to a shout above the cacophony of noise, disentangled himself from a svelte redhead and swept her up in his arms to kiss her.

Catherine smiled affectionately and gave him his present. 'Happy birthday, Nick.' Then, despite all her efforts, her eyes wandered past him, as she scanned the crowded room, annoyed with herself for the twinge of nervousness she felt. But she needn't have worried— Luke was nowhere to be seen, and neither was Mandy.

She danced, first with Nick, then with other partners,

out on the patio dance-floor, and still there was no sign of them. Each time the street door banged and a fresh crowd of guests burst in, Catherine's muscles tensed and she darted anxious looks but then, each time, she relaxed again. They weren't coming—surely everyone who was coming was here by now. They must have changed their minds—found something better to do. Her mind refused to contemplate what that something might be, and she told herself sternly that it was all to the good that they were missing. It would have been so easy, so tempting, to chicken out of the evening, to plead a bad headache, just to avoid them. But now there was no need and here she was, having a great time—in fact, it was almost like the old, carefree days.

She had finished a strenuous dance with a young man she dimly recollected from school and had sat down to chat animatedly with a couple of girls she also remembered, when she heard Nick's carrying voice. 'Hi, Luke, Hi, Mandy!' Catherine's heart plunged to her stomach and she shrank down in her chair, simultaneously cursing herself for being so stupid. She forced herself to seem nonchalant, casually picking up her glass in stiff fingers, before allowing herself to turn slightly towards the door.

Mandy, framed in the doorway, no doubt for maximum effect, was wearing a white dress which looked as though it had been made out of three or four men's handkerchiefs and very little else. She caught Catherine's eye across the room, gave her a swift look of smouldering antagonism then, before Catherine could avert her eyes, snuggled up closer to her companion. Luke—Catherine saw it with a sharp stab—was wearing pale blue, slim-fitting jeans and a white shirt, as usual making every other man, including Nick fade into obscurity.

She watched as Nick kissed Mandy then punched Luke's chest playfully. 'We'd given you up, man. Thought you were—otherwise occupied.' He grinned and nudged Luke, who merely smiled slightly.

Catherine turned her head away and realised that she was still clutching her glass, untasted. She sipped the punch, then carefully set it down and tried to pick up the threads of the lively discussion she had been having a couple of minutes earlier, but it was no use. Her face felt taut, like parchment stretched across a drum, and inside she felt only a dragging emptiness. Somehow, she smiled, even more brilliantly, she listened, she spoke when she had to, as her fingers listlessly clinked the ice cubes in her glass, and every few minutes she surreptitiously sneaked a glance at her watch, under cover of taking another sip. From her seat, she could see through an archway to the dimly lit dance-floor, where Mandy was giving a first-rate impression of a female octopus as she twined herself ever closer to Luke's lean body.

Somehow conscious that his eyes were on her, she hastily looked away, just as Nick pulled her to her feet for another dance. As the music slowly faded, one of the barmen appeared and hovered discreetly in the background. Nick kissed her ear. 'Don't go away, honey. I'll be right back—I just have to get some more drink up.'

He manoeuvred himself adroitly through the crowded room and disappeared in the direction of the cellar, leaving Catherine standing alone and rather uncertain. She peered at her watch again. Nearly midnight. The party would go on well into the early hours and she knew she ought to stay but that heavy listlessness still gripped her mind and body. Nick would probably not miss her—not for long, anyway. She would take the chance to slip away unseen.

'Ah, my gracious landlady. *My* dance, I think.'

Luke bowed ironically, and went to take her in his arms. Catherine stepped back, but he caught hold of her wrist.

'Let me go, you're hurting me,' she whispered, through her teeth, as he pulled her towards him. 'W-will you let me go! I don't want to dance with you,' she added, steeling herself to look up at him.

'But *I* want to dance with you,' he said, returning her look unsmilingly. Even in the dim light, she could see that his tanned face was deeply flushed and there was a kind of wild brilliance in his eyes. Too much rum, she thought. He had obviously had plenty before even arriving at the party. Her disgust was mingled with fear. Supposing he made an embarrassing scene, in front of everyone—how would she ever live it down? He put his arms round her and she willed herself not to resist.

'That's better.' His voice, just above her head, was softly mocking.

Catherine caught a glimpse of Mandy's hostile face. 'Your friend seems to think you should be dancing with her,' she remarked at the brown V of his chest, but he didn't even look in Mandy's direction as she retreated, sullen-faced, to the bar.

Luke was an excellent dancer and, almost without realising it, Catherine found her rigid body beginning to yield to his arms as they moved in rhythm to the slow, smoochy waltz. As though sensing her partial surrender, he drew her closer still, so that she could feel the heat from his firm body, and his warm breath as it stirred the tendrils of hair on her forehead. Her willpower seemed to be oozing out of her and she only felt a kind of drowsy elation at being in his arms . . .

But suddenly she jerked open her eyes. 'What did you say?'

'I said——' his voice was low, for her ears only '—I was sorry that you hadn't been for your rent this week.'

She tried to draw away, but his outspread fingers were tensed against the small of her back and she could only glare up at him.

'Don't you start that again!' she whispered fiercely.

'Why? It was a perfectly harmless remark. I'd thought we could take up where we left off the other afternoon.'

Catherine stumbled, then began trying unobtrusively to break his hold on her, but it was no use. He had her tightly, almost a prisoner, in his arms. Through stiff lips, she said coldly, 'I don't wish to dance with you any more. Will you stop, please.'

'Oh, I'm sure you don't really want me to.'

The open mockery in his voice grated on her. 'But I do,' she snapped, her voice rising slightly in spite of herself. They were dancing more and more slowly and Catherine, oblivious of the other couples around them, dragged herself back from his arms. 'I—I loathe you. Let me go—I don't want you to lay a finger on me ever again.'

His lips twitched with a derisory smile. 'I wouldn't be too sure of that, lady.'

They had given up all pretence of dancing now.

'W-what do you mean?' The words were out before she realised apprehensively that silence would have been wiser.

'What do I mean? Well, just think back to that afternoon, honey. If Mandy hadn't arrived, just in time to rescue me, well . . .'

Catherine gasped as a volatile and potent mixture of emotions—shame, misery and anger, compounded from all her encounters with this man—welled up from deep inside her then exploded.

'. . . so as for not laying a finger on you——'

The blow, delivered without conscious thought, struck him across the face, so that he rocked back on his heels for a moment. The sound was like a pistol shot and it shocked Catherine, who was almost beside herself, into consciousness of just where she was—at the centre of a highly interested circle of spectators. Even the steel band had momentarily stopped playing, as though acknowledging that their music was temporarily of minor interest.

The anger had all gone with the blow, but the shame and misery now flooded through her, so that she could have sunk to her knees. Instead, she clenched her shaking hands together, feeling the palm of her right hand sting where she had struck him and, without giving him another glance, she thrust her way off the dance-floor and through to the bar, snatched up her bag and, totally unable to focus on any individual face, wrenched open the door. For a few minutes she leaned unsteadily against her car, taking deep gulps of the cool night air, then, terrified that Nick—or someone else—might follow her, she got in and somehow drove herself home.

She was still wide awake and staring, dull-eyed, at her bedroom ceiling, when the phone rang, the shrill tone echoing through the silent house. She leapt out of bed and stumbled down the passage, afraid that it would disturb Mattie, before she remembered that she was away for the weekend for her niece's wedding over at Frenchy's Bay.

'Cathy, honey—what happened to you?' Nick's voice, slightly slurred, was warm with concern.

'Oh, Nick, I'm sorry. I should have said goodbye. It's just—it's just that I was very tired suddenly. I've been working very hard for Aunt Lu this week,' she lied plausibly, praying that Nick was not aware of the shameful manner of her leaving, but her heart sank when he said,

'And what exactly went on between Luke and you? If he's upset you——'

'Oh, well——' she stammered lamely '—you know how these things blow up——'

'But I want to know, honey. You were one of my guests, so—what did he do?'

His voice was bellicose and Catherine leaned her head wearily against the panelled wall. Nick's pose, acting as the affronted mine host, was just one thing more than she could bear, on top of everything else. She gave a faint sigh.

'All right, Nick, he—he insulted me.'

There was a muffled explosion of anger at the other
end of the line and she went on quickly, 'No, Nick, you
mustn't blame yourself for inviting him or anything like
that. Please, just forget it. It's just that Luke Devinish
and I—well, we've crossed swords before, and
tonight——'

'How come?'

'Well—there are reasons.' Suddenly, the desire to tell
all, to unburden herself to just this one old friend, who
she knew would be sympathetic, was overwhelming.
'You see, I own some of the land out at Coral Strand that
Brannan are interested in.'

'Brannan?'

Catherine had a momentary flicker of surprise. Surely
Nick knew all about it?

'Yes—you know, Brannan International.'

'Brannan International!' Nick's voice shook with
excitement. 'Opening up here? Good God, Cathy, this
could be the making of St Hilaire!'

'Yes. They've made this marvellous offer for it, but I
can't sell because he's squatting on it and he says he won't
leave.'

'Oh, won't he?'

'No. We've tried—but please, Nick,' too late, her
sense of caution resurfaced, 'I only told you because——'

'He'll have to be removed!'

'What?'

'Luke—he'll have to go. Just you leave all this to me,
honey.' There was a hard edge to his voice which she had
never heard before.

'Leave all w-what to you? What do you mean, Nick?'

'Why—persuading your squatter to leave, of course.
I'll get Carl to pay him a visit.'

Catherine realised, with a chill, that Nick was already
referring to Luke, not by name, but as 'he' and 'your
squatter'.

'Carl?' she faltered.

'Sure. You've seen him, haven't you?'

Carl? Oh, yes, she'd seen him all right. Nick's minder—that terrifying hulk whom she had seen several times hanging around the Lord Nelson, looking as though he had lurched his way out of a James Bond movie. She ran her tongue over her dry lips.

'Yes,' Nick's cool voice was reflective, 'Carl's the man. He can be very—persuasive when he wants to be. Pity, but we can't let one pig-headed squatter stand between us and all those lovely dollar bills, can we? I'm leaving for Caracas first thing, on business, but I'll see Carl before I go. Better still, he can take some of his friends.' Then, as Catherine made an incoherent sound, he went on firmly, 'And you're not to worry your beautiful little head about it any more, sweetheart. Just you leave it to Nick, and I promise that by this time tomorrow——' Catherine heard a woman's voice, then Nick laughed and said, 'Must go now, honey, 'Bye——'

'No, Nick, no—please don't——' Catherine's voice was sharp with urgency but he had rung off.

She replaced the receiver with shaking hands and went into the lounge. Not bothering to switch on the light, she hunched in the sofa, her knees under her chin, as she stared out through the dark outline of window, contemplating the enormity of what she had done.

Summer lightning was flickering far out to sea, beyond Coral Strand . . . Coral Strand . . . Luke—unaware, quite unknowing . . . Catherine swallowed hard. But, after all, why should she worry? It was surely no more than he deserved, after the appalling way he had treated her. She would get back to bed, go to sleep, and by the time she woke in the morning it would all be over. Let Carl do her dirty work for her. Why not? Let him achieve at a stroke what Uncle Bob had been too squeamish even to consider. Perhaps, confronted with Carl and his cohorts, Luke would go quietly. But no—she knew that he was not the kind of man to give in without a struggle. He simply wouldn't know how to ... The sudden image of Luke, strong and athletic as he undoubtedly was, matched against Nick's henchmen made her shudder. No, there had to be another way. The court case was coming up in a few days, when surely he would be evicted lawfully. Whatever reasons she might have for wishing him away, out of her life, once and for all, she must not let it happen this way!

Immediately, she was on her feet and running to her bedroom. She pulled on a dress, almost screaming with impatience as the tie belt caught round her shoulders, snatched up her car keys and hurled herself through the front door, slamming it behind her.

Dawn was just breaking as the car hurtled off the main road, down the uneven track and came to a halt. Hurry, hurry—she must get there first! She pushed her way through the scrub bushes, which caught against her dress and scratched her arms. The cabin was just ahead of her in the half-light, the door slightly ajar. Catherine put her hand against it, then stopped, frozen by a sudden thought. Supposing Luke was not alone—supposing Mandy was with him. She closed her eyes for a moment, fighting against the sick feeling that threatened to engulf her, then she steeled herself. He must be warned and the risk of seeing Mandy—in his arms perhaps—her coldly triumphant eyes, was a small price to pay. She pushed against the door and it moved slightly as she cleared her throat nervously.

'H-hello. Anyone there?'

There was no reply, not even when she pushed the door wide open. He wasn't there. So he *was* with Mandy—at her place. Well, at least that would keep him out of Carl's reach for a while. Catherine knew she should be relieved but the feeling resembled much more overwhelming misery. Her hand dropped by her side and she turned to leave, when her sharp ears caught, from the cabin, a faint noise, almost a groan.

Not allowing herself to hesitate any longer, she stepped inside. By the faint light which filtered in she could see Luke, bare-chested but still wearing the jeans of the previous evening. He was lying hunched on his side on an old mattress, his head on his arm, and with an enormous surge of relief she saw that he was quite alone. She said again, 'Hello,' but he did not stir. Then, as she stood looking down at him irresolutely, he groaned again and flung himself on to his other side, his arm brushing across her legs, to flop on to the floor.

Her face hardened. He was drunk—blind drunk. Of course; what a little innocent she had been to think he would be otherwise. She remembered, all too clearly, his face the previous evening, flushed, glittering-eyed—and that was when he had arrived at the party. He must have been drinking steadily, even before that. She stared down at the huddled shape. What a fool she was! Well, as of this minute, she was going to be a fool no longer. She would leave him to whatever fate was coming to him, and good riddance!

She swung on her heel, but then stopped with her hand on the door post, her thumb picking at a splinter of wood, then very slowly she turned back again. Well, he *is* a human being, she told her mocking inner voice fiercely, and I can't just stand by and see him hurt.

She knelt down beside him, and then her brain registered what it had been struggling to grasp since she had first entered the hut. There was no smell of liquor, not the faintest whiff of rum, and surely, she reasoned, there should be. She put her face right down to his but there was only the tang of sweat. He groaned again and Catherine's heart turned over. She was too late—Carl and his friends had already paid their visit. She put a tentative hand against his face, searching for signs of bruising, then gasped with shock. His forehead was burning hot. When she gently moved her hand down, his neck and chest were soaked in perspiration, blast waves of heat coming from his body. She felt for his pulse and his whole arm throbbed under the pressure of her fingers.

She sat back on her heels, chewing her lip. His hectic flush, those brilliant eyes, now the fever—they added up to just one thing. He was not drunk; he had denghi fever—or crack-bone, as the locals so appositely called it. Whatever could she do? She dared not leave him— sooner or later, Nick's followers would arrive. And anyway—her eyes swept round the cabin, immaculately clean and tidy, but bare of the least necessity such as running water—he desperately needed looking after for the thirty-six hours or so that the fever would rage. The Public Hospital? No, he was not ill enough—they certainly would not admit him. She must take him home, she thought, telling herself stoutly that sentiment did not in the least enter into it. He was simply a human being in need of help.

First, she must wrap him up, or he would get pneumonia and save Nick a job. An old sweater was lying nearby—the very one that he had fetched for her, but she forced that painful memory from her mind. She knelt behind him and, putting her hands under his arms, somehow dragged him to a sitting position. In spite of his incoherent protests, she managed to get him into the sweater then, as if exhausted, he laid his head against her breast, his cheek blazing hot through her cotton dress. Catherine looked down at the dark head and something caught in her throat painfully. Hardly aware of what she was doing, she smoothed back his untidy hair. Her arms tightened round him as a feeling of immense tenderness welled up inside her then, almost terrified at her temerity, she dropped a hurried, guilty kiss on to the ruffled hair.

It was a dreadful struggle, first to get him shakily on to his feet, protesting angrily, then out to the car. She had driven in as close as she could but even so, bearing most of his weight, it was almost more than she could manage before finally, somehow, he was heaved into the vehicle.

On the back seat of her baby car Luke was all arms and legs, but at least he was in.

It was full daylight now, as she raced home, almost as though Carl were snapping at her very heels, but it was still very early so there was a heavy silence over the town and the road up to Hope's Mill was deserted. As she drove, her brain was very active. What room shall I put him in? Damn, the spare-room beds aren't made up . . . He'll have to go in mine, it's the only one with a mosquito net . . . What a good thing Mattie's away. She'd only fuss . . . I can look after him perfectly well on my own . . .

After another brief struggle, Luke was stretched out on her wide bed, his head on her pillow, his eyes closed in exhaustion and his whole body gleaming with sweat. Suddenly, the enormity of just what she was doing struck Catherine for the first time. A sick man—sick enough to need all sorts of intimate ministrations—and she was quite alone with him, she thought with sudden apprehension. Perhaps it wasn't too late, even now, to try the Public Hospital? Oh, for goodness' sake, she thought, get a hold of yourself. What would Mum think of you? In spite of herself, a warm smile broke briefly across her face and she seemed to hear her mother's brisk voice. 'There's nothing to worry about, Cathy. After all, one naked man's pretty much the same as all the rest, give or take a few extra pounds dotted here and there!'

First, she must get him out of those tight jeans and into something cool. She frowned in thought, then went to the chest of drawers and rummaged around until she found what she was searching for—a pair of old beach pyjamas that one summer, when she was about fifteen, had been *the* indispensable item of Port Charlotte teenage *haute couture*. She shook them out and held them up. Baggy, lightweight Madras cotton—yes, they would be fine, and she would just about be able to squeeze Luke's lean frame into them. Quite how he would react when he was recovered sufficiently to register the tasteful shades of fuchsia and lime was another matter, but that was by the way for now.

She fetched a bowl of cool water and, kneeling on the bed beside him, dragged off the sweater and began gently sponging his hot face, then his chest and arms. She was just wiping his palm when, without warning, his eyes opened and he looked straight at her.

'Cattie?'

'It's all right, Luke,' she whispered.

'God, I feel bloody.' He tried to sit up, then put his hand to his head and fell back on the pillow. 'What the hell's going on?' There was a faint touch of the old asperity in his voice, and Catherine put her hand gently over his mouth.

'Ssh, don't try to talk. You've got denghi fever.'

He closed his eyes wearily and turned his head away with a groan. She finished washing him then took a deep breath and with unsteady fingers unzipped his jeans and pulled them off, deeply grateful that he knew neither where he was nor what was going on. In spite of all his efforts to the contrary, eventually she got him into the pyjamas, but his struggles wore him out and he rolled on to his side and fell into a heavy sleep.

Catherine knelt beside the bed, looking down at him, a strange, totally new feeling inside her. This was her enemy—a man who took a savage delight in thwarting her, hurting her, at every turn, who, just a few hours previously, had insulted and degraded her. And yet, he lay, his face pillowed on his hand, his long dark lashes hiding those cynical grey eyes, the strain lines etched round his mouth as though from constantly disciplining himself now smoothed and softened by sleep. With a strange, fluttering sensation, she lifted her hand and trailed one finger lightly across his lips, then, outraged at her behaviour, she sprang to her feet and went off, almost angrily, to shower and change. She put on a severe navy shirt-waister, tied back her hair into a no-nonsense knot, and somehow felt much more in control of the situation . . .

She had intended to spend the day reading on the veranda, within call, but Luke, after his initial sleep, was so restless and unwell that she gave up and sat in the room with him, only leaving to get herself a hasty snack. In spite of having every door and louvre in the house propped wide open, for a cooling draught, he was red-hot with fever, groaning and tossing constantly. Catherine, who had had crack-bone herself, saw him suffer with sympathy, knowing that his head, every bone and joint in his body was aching as though it had been wrenched asunder. She sponged him down, ignoring his irritable mutterings, then lifted his head on her arm and forced sips of weak fruit juice past his dry lips, all the time without his showing any further sign of recognition.

At last, by late evening, when she looked down at him by the dim light of her bedside lamp, she could see that he was a little better. His forehead, although still hot, was not so clammy and he was less restless. She stripped off his pyjamas, which were wringing wet—this time without any mumbled protests from him—washed him thoroughly and put on a clean pair in shocking pink and hot orange stripes. Then, after covering him carefully with the sheet and, draping the mosquito shroud down over the bed, she tiptoed out and made herself a welcome meal of cold meat and salad.

But there was one thing more that she had to do, something that had twinged on and off all day, like toothache. Taking the phone from the hall into the lounge, so as not to disturb Luke, she rang the Lord Nelson and managed to make Carl understand, speaking very firmly and incisively, that Nick did not, after all, want Luke dealt with and that not a hair on his head was to be harmed. And that's that, she thought, quietly replacing the receiver. When Luke had recovered—well, it would be up to him.

Afterwards, she showered and put on her nightie, then carried the old padded mattress from the chaise-longue into her bedroom; with a couple of sheets, it would make a comfortable enough bed. Luke was still asleep—quite peacefully, it seemed, in the moonlight—but the sheet was tangled at his feet so she tucked it more firmly then lay down on her mattress. Mmm, it's been quite a day, she thought, as she closed her eyes, quite a day . . .

Just as she was sinking gratefully into sleep, the mosquitoes arrived—hundreds of them, it seemed—and Catherine wailed inwardly. The town, particularly the small tourist area, was sprayed not too irregularly but up here people took their chance against the ravening hordes and she knew that, having discovered her, they would be zooming in at her all night long. She felt one nip her forehead and swatted angrily at it. Perhaps if she carried the mattress into the bathroom and closed the louvres and door tightly . . . But huge cockroaches sometimes came scuttling up through the plughole. She swallowed at the thought.

She heard Luke tossing and got up to find he was yet again uncovered and now his body felt quite chilled. She pulled the sheet over him again, just as another mosquito whined close to her ear. Her heart sank to the floorboards. No sleep the previous night, running back and forth to Luke all day—she was exhausted. What was she to do? And that mosquito net was quite wasted. She knew from long experience that anyone else in the room with *her* would be quite safe, in fact, remain unmolested all night, while she was devoured. She looked down almost resentfully at Luke, who was now sleeping like a baby. A mosquito landed on her arm and, without daring to allow herself further thought, she climbed carefully on to the bed and under the sheet, pulled the net down into place and curled up on the extreme edge of the bed.

Luke was perfectly still, his breathing quite regular, but for some time Catherine lay rigid, her heart palpitating uncomfortably against her ribs, as strange emotions warred inside her—fear, uncertainty and yes— although she strove to push it away from her, a warm feeling that gradually pervaded her. This was how it would be to be married to Luke, to lie beside him every night, secure in his nearness. She smiled into the darkness, closed her eyes and relaxed . . .

She sprang into wakefulness, her eyes wide open. Luke had rolled up against her, an arm and leg sprawled possessively across her body.

'Darling.' His voice was thick with sleep.

Horrifed, she resisted her impulse to leap out of bed and tried to extricate herself with extreme caution but even as she moved his weight came down more heavily on her.

'Don't leave me. You *must* stay.'

Catherine, who was in the act of wriggling backwards, stopped dead at the bleak desolation in his voice, moved by the pain so apparent in his tone. Shifting her position slightly, she gazed down at his face, a sombre mask of unhappiness in the pale moonlight. And mask was right, she thought all at once, for no one could ever guess what lay behind that normally cynical, aloof face.

Who was the woman whom Luke, in his fever, was appealing to? And what could she have done to arouse such a depth of feeling in him? Was she—Catherine forced herself to face the question—was she his wife? Or—her heart leapt for an instant—had his marriage failed, ending in separation or divorce? Was this the real reason why he had appeared from nowhere, cutting himself loose from all ties with his past? Had she been wrong, after all? Was his war with Brannan just a side issue, a bonus, giving a spurious sense of purpose to his aimless, drifter's existence? Perhaps one day, she thought, she would learn the truth—or would this enigmatic man remain for ever, for her at least, an enigma?

Her slight, almost furtive movement had disturbed him. He murmured in protest and his hand curved over her shoulder, as though trying to hold her to him. She put her free arm gently round him.

'Ssh, it's all right,' she whispered, then added softly, 'Don't worry—I'll stay with you.' But she knew, with a pang, that Luke, in his half-delirious state, was quite unaware of *her* presence—he had been speaking to someone else entirely. After a few minutes, he relaxed his hold, but Catherine lay a while longer, feeling his warm breath on her bare arm, before she too drifted off to sleep.

The distant sound of church bells was drifting into the room; the sunshine was brilliant against her closed eyelids. Catherine rolled over on to her back, stretching herself like a cat, then stiffened in shock as memory flooded back. Very slowly, she turned her head, to see Luke's grey eyes, no longer brilliant with fever, fixed on her. She made an instinctive movement away from him, bracing herself for his caustic comments, but they never came. Instead, he put his hand lightly across her stomach.

'Don't go. I like you here.'

His voice, although clear, was weak and she easily brushed off his hand. 'Yes, yes,' she babbled. 'I must get up. I—I only came in because of the mosquitoes. I'll have a shower.'

She ducked quickly under the net, snatched up her housecoat and clothes and almost ran out of the room. After her shower, she put on the same navy dress, scragged her hair into an even more severe knot and, for extra effect, added one of Mattie's voluminous white aprons. When she went back to the bedroom he smiled lazily up at her as she set down the bowl of water, but then, as she lifted him up on the pillow, he tried ineffectually to push her away.

'Leave me alone. I'm all right. What the hell's going on, anyway?'

She squeezed out the sponge and mopped his face thoroughly. 'You've had denghi fever. I couldn't leave you in your hut—so I brought you back here.'

'Hut? What were you doing in my hut?'

She dried his face, as he turned it irritably on the pillow, then, summoning up her courage, knelt down beside him and, in a few words, told him about Nick's phone call. There was no reaction from him, so she said urgently, 'Luke, do you understand what I'm saying?'

'Of course I understand you. I'm not a bloody idiot!' he grumbled. He tried to lift himself off the pillow but lay back with a groan. 'God, I feel lousy!'

Catherine, looking at his pale face, stood up. 'You need some food. Have a rest, while I get you some breakfast.'

'Don't want any breakfast.'

'Oh yes, you do,' she said brightly, turning as she went out of the door to see him feebly punching the pillow.

In the kitchen, she prepared a thick slice of paw paw, juicy and golden, then she put on the coffee-pot, lightly boiled an egg and cut dainty fingers of toast. Luke was half asleep when she returned but she woke him, hoisted him on to the pillow and then, as he seemed too indolent to move, dipped a piece of toast into the egg.

'Come on, open wide—soldiers.'

He ate it obediently but scowled up at her.

'You're really enjoying this, aren't you?'

'Enjoying what?' She returned his look, her eyes innocent and guileless, and shoved in another slice of toast.

'Bossing me,' he snarled thickly. 'And as for these monstrosities,' he picked at the beach pyjamas irritably, 'if I didn't feel as weak as a baby, I'd——'

'Black or white coffee?' she enquired sweetly, and he subsided again.

After breakfast, he went straight off to sleep again but by midday he was awake and looking much better.

'Would you like some soup for lunch?' she asked, and he grunted an assent. Huh, not much improvement temper-wise, she thought.

'There's beef broth, minestrone, lentil, spring vegetable, cream of chicken—that would be nice, wouldn't it?' she said cajolingly but he gave her an imperious frown.

'Tomato—I only like tomato soup.'

Oh, wouldn't you just, thought Catherine, aware of the absence of tomato soup from Mattie's dry goods larder, but she bit back her tongue. He's an invalid, remember, she told herself.

'Beef broth would be more nourishing——' she began but he snapped, 'Tomato, or nothing!' and turned over away from her.

There was a little shanty store at the bottom of the hill, open most of the night and on Sundays as well.

'OK,' she said. 'But I'll have to get the car out to fetch you some.'

She bent to smooth the crumpled sheet and caught his eye.

'You'd make a good nurse, Miss Nightingale.' He gave her a faint, almost shamefaced smile, so that Catherine's busy hands stilled for a moment, then she smiled back.

'Well—my mother was a nurse. Perhaps it runs in the blood, like blue eyes.'

'Do they live in England, your parents?'

She finished tucking in the sheet. 'No. They were both killed in a car crash, when I was at school. They were in England on a recruiting trip—and to see me, of course.'

She didn't meet his eyes and was turning to leave, when he caught her wrist.

'That's tough.' He spoke slowly, almost to himself. 'I didn't know that, Catherine.'

There was something, a softness, in his voice that she had never heard before and this, combined with his use of her name, made her catch her breath for a moment. To cover up, she smiled brightly down at him and withdrew her hand.

'Oh, there's a lot you don't know about me. Now, I must get that soup—I shan't be long.'

She bought the last three tins of tomato soup and, with a vague idea that Luke needed lots of carbohydrates, a packet of sticky, yellow buns. As she walked back into the kitchen, she realised with astonishment that she felt light-hearted, even happy. All the resentment and anger towards Luke had disappeared and she only had a tremendous yearning to care for him, look after him. Horrified, she caught herself up and, thrusting these disturbing feelings away from her, put the soup on to heat and prepared the rest of his lunch. If he was well enough, it would do him good to sit out on the veranda in the afternoon breeze, so she put an armful of cushions into one of the cane chairs and dragged an old table across.

When his meal was ready, she went through to the bedroom. 'Luke, if I help you, would you like——' But the words died on her lips. The bed was empty, so was the room. He must have gone to the bathroom, perhaps for a shower. The bathroom door, though, was wide open, its cool tiled interior undisturbed.

Catherine returned slowly to the bedroom. She saw now what she had somehow known she would see—that Luke's clothes, his sweater and jeans, which she had left hanging over a chair, had gone. In their place, neatly folded, were the beach pyjamas and a piece of cream paper, torn hastily from her notepad which lay on the dressing-table. She unfolded it, very carefully, as though it might break. The scrawled words jumbled in front of her eyes and she had to read them several times before they sank in. 'Thanks a lot, Cattie. See you.'

She sat down on the edge of the bed, the emptiness washing through her like a grey tide. She put her hand down, and fancied that the crumpled sheet still bore the

warmth of his body. He had gone. Without waiting for
her, without even a word of thanks, apart from the
briefest of notes. Not that she wanted thanks, but it
would have shown that he too wanted something at least
a little different in their relationship. As it was—her
mouth twisted with pain—he couldn't even wait until he
was well to get away, to distance himself from her, to
show her coldly and deliberately that nothing had
changed.

Tears of disappointment welled up in her eyes; she
sniffed and brushed her cheek, as one hot tear
overflowed. Then she heaved a sigh, got up very slowly
and went back to the kitchen. There was no point in
wasting good food. She poured the tomato soup into a
bowl and carried it carefully out on to the veranda.

CHAPTER SIX

CATHERINE turned off the outboard motor and dragged the dinghy on to the shelving beach. She straightened up and looked around her, thinking, with a mixture of contentment and relief, that everything was just as she remembered it. Mangrove Cay was exactly as it had been when it was a favourite picnic place for her and her parents—a tiny, wooded island, fringed by a band of pure white sand, two miles off-shore from St Hilaire. A deserted island, an empty beach, all to herself—sunbathing, swimming, a picnic lunch for one, then home in good time to change for the hearing.

The hearing! The mere thought of it sent butterflies fluttering round in her stomach. The last few days—and nights—had been unbearably hot, no doubt brewing up for the summer rains, and last night the combination of clammy, humid air and stretched nerves had driven away all hopes of sleep, so she had seized on this brainwave of an early-morning excursion to Mangrove Cay as a means of calming her overwrought mind.

Bliss, pure bliss, she thought, as she dropped her towel and beach bag on to the sand and gazed out over the shimmering sea, where a solitary fishing-boat was making its slow way across the far horizon. But then her eye caught the silver gleam of an airliner, banking before making its final run. That would be the New York flight—the Brannan officials would be on board, ready to sign the contract if—no, when—the hearing went their way. The hearing—she must get it out of her mind!

She peeled off her blouse and shorts, which were clammy-tight against her skin, then reached for her bikini. With her hand on it, though, she paused. Apart from the lone fishing-boat, nothing was visible, and anyway, she thought, no one, unless they were seeking shelter during a storm, ever came here. Not allowing herself to hesitate any longer, she dropped her bikini on to her towel and ran down the beach, gasping with delight at the feel of the waves against her bare skin. She swam for a long time, revelling in the freedom of her body cleaving through the limpid, silky water, then rolled over on to her back. The sun was quite high in the sky. She must get out now, dry off, then have her lunch and leave—she would never hear the end of it from Uncle Bob if she was late or, at the very least, arrived with wet hair. She smiled to herself as she remembered his final injunction—'And remember, Cathy, be sure and wear a *hat*!'

She was swimming lazily back towards shallow water when her stomach muscles suddenly tightened in shocked alarm. A man was standing at the water's edge, his hard, dark outline somehow menacing against the soft greens and golds of the island. The instinct of alarm was followed by an immediate spasm of rage as she recognised Luke Devinish.

She hastily ducked down and trod water as he lifted a casual hand. 'Hi, Cat.'

'What are you doing here?' Shock and exasperation mingled in her voice.

'Tch, tch. That's not very friendly—or do you own Mangrove Cay as well?'

Catherine cursed herself inwardly for the malignant demon which had tempted her to do a pre-hearing victory roll across the bay, instead of avoiding the Coral Strand area as though it were a plague zone. He must have seen her and followed her out here.

Her lips tightened and a spot of angry colour burned high on her cheeks. Yet again, *yet* again, he was intruding, thrusting his way in where he was not wanted. Under the shock of seeing him, she had momentarily

forgotten their last meeting, but now, with the memory of
his casual disappearance and—more—the shame she
still felt at her treacherous feelings for him returning, she
felt a kind of panic run through her. She had to get away
from this man! She began to swim rapidly away from the
beach but soon tired and turned round—to see him still
watching her.

'Well—are you intending to stay out there all day? In
that case——'

To Catherine's horror, he pulled off his T-shirt and,
tossing it down on her towel, waded in, then struck out
towards her. For a split second, she just stared at him,
then, recovering her wits, she began swimming blindly
away from him.

'Hey, Cat,' his voice was just behind her, 'are you
planning on swimming to Mexico?'

She turned her head and saw, with a flicker of fear,
that the shore had retreated alarmingly. She swung away
again and began swimming towards the beach but he
caught up with her again and swam easily alongside her,
watching her with a malicious glint in his eye.

'G-go away,' she gasped, but he just shook his head at
her sadly.

'What an unoriginal mind you have. All you ever say to
me is "go away".'

A wave caught her, so that she bobbed like a cork and
began paddling desperately to keep herself under water,
at the same time casting a despairing look at her clothes,
arranged in a neat mound on the beach.

'L-look,' she spluttered urgently, 'I haven't got a——'

'—swimsuit on. Oh, that's quite obvious. And
anyway,' his smile was provoking, 'what's an itsy-witsy
bikini between friends?'

She turned a stormy face towards him.

'If you were a gentleman you'd go away.' Her anger
was increased by the faintly pathetic note that had
entered her voice.

'But I'm not a gentleman. Remember? You're always telling me that. Still, as a special favour, and as I quite appreciate that you're capable of paddling around in ever decreasing circles for the next three hours or more, I'll close my eyes—just while I count to ten, you understand. One——'

Catherine tore through the shallows, fell headlong, picked herself up and stumbled across to her towel. With trembling fingers, she wrapped herself in it sarong-style, then realised that—her bikini was missing.

'Where is it?' she demanded fiercely as Luke sauntered up to her. 'What have you done with it?'

He eyed her for a moment, as though scientifically assessing just how much further he could provoke her. Then he gestured with his head and she saw her pink bikini dangling from the branch of a tree—just out of reach of her outstretched hand. Desperately, she jumped up at it but then, as her towel slipped, she clutched it to her and beat her fist against the trunk in frustration. She looked round for a piece of wood—anything—to hook it down, but there was nothing. Her temper was smouldering. But she made an effort to control herself—nothing would please Luke more than to see her hopping around in a wild fury. Leaving the bikini to its fate, she snatched up her clothes and retreated behind a clump of bushes, where, almost too angry to dry herself, she dragged on her blouse and shorts.

When she emerged, her hair still dripping, he was sprawling at his ease, tossing pebbles into the fringe of foam that rolled along the beach, but as she appeared he lay back, his hands linked behind his head and his eyes closed. She flung her unused suntan oil and book into her bag, trying to ignore his presence, but against her will her eyes were drawn to his lean, brown frame, still gleaming with water drops like the pelt of a sea animal . . . his wet denim shorts moulded to his body . . . his thin, suntanned face, the dark hair overshadowing his grey eyes—

which were watching her. She blushed in confusion as her eyes met his then slid away. She snatched up the big velvety red and blue beach towel and began folding it with geometric precision.

'You seem to have made a complete recovery,' she said coldly, giving the towel a final exact fold.

'Oh—it must be the excellent nursing I had.'

He smiled up at her, a seemingly genuine smile, and Catherine was momentarily perplexed. Constantly wary of him, she did not quite know how to take this remark and suddenly she wanted desperately to know why he had gone that day. She opened her mouth to ask but then, as her pride got the better of this weakness, she closed it without uttering a word. Don't be more of a fool than you have to be, she told herself scornfully. That would only give him the chance to insult her in some way—no doubt, he was just biding his opportunity. No, she must not on any account allow him to suspect how he had hurt her—that would be madness.

'Oh, anyone would have done the same, I'm sure,' she said off-handedly.

'Such as?'

'Well—Mandy, for one. She'd have been only too delighted to bathe your fevered brow, and——' She broke off.

'And? Share a bed with me, you mean?' He slanted a sideways look at her.

'No, I didn't. Although, since you mention it, no doubt she would—if she hasn't done so already!' she burst out, then bit her lip. She was getting involved in a verbal sparring match again—and they always ended the same way! As she bent to pick up her bag Luke put his hand on her wrist.

'Not jealous, surely? Not of the delectable Mandy?'

Catherine tried to wrench her hand away. 'Jealous?' Her laugh was imbued with all the scorn she could muster. 'Of Mandy—and all the other empty-headed females who seem to collapse at your feet at a look from the great Casanova? Hardly. Anyway—to be jealous of them, I'd have to feel something for you, wouldn't I— that is, apart from downright detestation.'

She made a snatch at her bag, anxious now to retreat out of reach, but his grip on her wrist only tightened, encircling it in a band of steel.

'And just where are you off to in such a hurry?'

She glared at him. 'You know perfectly well where. It's the hearing—don't tell me you'd forgotten?'

'Oh yes, so it is.' He was grinning openly now and Catherine felt a momentary shiver of disquiet. He increased the pressure on her wrist until she was forced down relentlessly on to the sand beside him. 'It's not too late, you know.'

'Not too late—for what?'

'To save you from making a fool of yourself.'

'You don't know what you're talking about,' she said coldly. 'And will you please let go of my wrist?'

'Not just yet.' He turned to face her. 'You're not going to win this case. Whatever you might think about it, the law's on my side. So why not be sensible and call the whole thing off?'

She looked at him in amazement and saw that his expression was deadly serious.

'Call it off? At this stage? You can't mean it! And as for us losing, Uncle Bob says——'

'"Uncle Bob says!"' he mimicked savagely. 'I wouldn't rely too heavily on his judgement, if I were you. Other people can read law books as well as that old——'

'I've told you—keep Uncle Bob out of this!' Catherine's face was white with fury.

'OK—but just tell me this, Cattie. Supposing, by some gross miscarriage of justice, you do win today, are you still determined to get the ink on the contract with Brannan just as fast as you possibly can?'

Catherine just managed to suppress the involuntary

start. Could Luke possibly have got wind of the meeting arranged for the next morning? That could be disastrous—but, surely news of that, at least, had not leaked out? Nevertheless, she could not be certain—she would have to guard her words very carefully.

'We shall certainly be signing with them, yes, as and when it suits us,' she said, injecting as much firmness into her tone as she could muster.

'Oh, of course,' his tone was angry now, 'you just won't be able to wait a moment longer than you have to, to get your hands on all those lovely dollar bills!'

Catherine bit back the hot retort that sprang to her lips. How easily, she thought, she could wipe the sneer from his face by telling him about her plans for the hospital. But pride kept her silent. Why should she grovel to him, in an effort to win his good opinion? And anyway, in his present mood, he wouldn't believe her. He had clearly chosen to cast her in the part of the greedy, mercenary villain—and he would not be willing to allow her to change that role.

'But why does it have to be with Brannan?' To her utter amazement, there was an expression almost of pleading in his eyes, as if he was willing her to contradict him. 'If you are so absolutely determined to go through with this, why won't you even consider selling to anyone else?'

What on earth was his devious mind getting at now?

'But there isn't anyone else. If there were, well, we would have considered their offer, of course.'

'Isn't anyone else?' He sounded genuinely astonished, then seemed to recover himself swiftly. 'I'll say this for you, Cattie, you're a damned good actress with that wide-eyed innocent look of yours. You nearly had me fooled for a moment.'

'Just what are you talking about?' Catherine's mind was whirling with bewilderment.

'Of course there's been another bid. It's just that that

pig-headed uncle of yours refused point blank to consider it.' He eyed her narrowly. 'He must have told you about it.'

'No, he didn't,' she retorted. 'And he most certainly would have done. Why should I believe a word you're saying? I trust Uncle Bob—and I don't trust you! You're just trying it on again, aren't you—trying to undermine us? You've been intent on causing trouble ever since you arrived on St Hilaire. But I tell you this, you'll never succeed in coming between me and Uncle Bob—never!' She drew a deep breath. 'Now, will you let me go?'

Without a word he loosed her wrist and spread wide his hands. 'OK, honey, have it your way. Off you go.'

Catherine could hardly believe it. She had won! For the first time in all her encounters with Luke Devinish, she had won—if not the war, at least this skirmish. With a feeling of bubbling jubilation, she seized her bag and without another glance at him strode down the beach to the dinghy, slid it down into the water and scrambled in.

She pulled at the starter cord but there was no response. She tugged again—and again, with increasing urgency, but the engine remained stubbornly lifeless. She leaned her head down on her knee. Mackenzie, the boatman, had assured her that her boat had been thoroughly overhauled, but obviously it had not been done quite well enough. What was she to do? She had to get back to Port Charlotte! Panic rippled through her, then she thought of Luke. He must have come by boat and would be going back soon. Well, he could give her a lift. After all, despite their recent angry words, he did owe her some sort of favour, surely.

She looked up, trying to mould her face into a becoming humility, then her eyes widened with disbelief. Luke, still lolling on the beach, was holding up for her inspection a sparking plug. Instinctively, she knew. The motor was not broken—*he* had disabled it!

As she leapt out of the boat and went towards him,

with great deliberation he thrust the plug into his shorts pocket.

'G-give me that!' Catherine held out her hand to him, but in response he merely shook his head at her.

'I had hoped that you'd be willing to listen to reason, but I rather feared you'd be as stubborn as ever. So I had to take—precautions.'

He looked at her, with that old half-mocking, half-sardonic smile, then deliberately turned his head away. A fleeting, bitter memory of that dark head on her breast flooded through her then ebbed, leaving her angrier than ever, and she launched herself at him. She had the advantage of surprise and they both fell sideways in a tangled heap, her full weight against him.

As he struggled to extricate himself, her hand closed on the plug and with a gasp of triumph she jerked it free and made her escape. But Luke's hard hand was on her ankle, a swift tug and, with a yelp, she fell all over him again. This time he had the advantage and he pinned her to him with one arm so that she could not struggle and with the other hand began to wrench open her fingers. She hit him a glancing blow and he caught her hand, his grip tightening on it.

'Stop it,' he said sternly, 'or I'll have to hurt you.'

She fought fiercely against him and in reply, he shook her.

'Behave, will you! I haven't harmed you yet, and I don't want to——'

Crimson-faced and panting, Catherine swore at him and he laughed, so that she felt his laughter all through her.

'Dear, dear—and I thought you were such a little lady. Now, behave, or I'll——' He left the threat unfinished and loosed his grip.

Catherine decided reluctantly that discretion was the better part of valour and sat back between her heels, glaring at him through her tumbled hair.

'You—you did hurt me,' she said.

'No, I didn't, and you know it. If anything, I was on the receiving end.' He touched the side of his jaw where her fist had caught him a flailing blow and rubbed it tenderly. 'I shall obviously have to rename you,' he went on, considering, 'Cat is much too domesticated, too tame. Those eyes, that temper -Tiger is more fitting, I think. Yes—that suits you perfectly. It sounds like one of those eighteenth-century bruisers—twenty rounds with Battling Tiger Hartley. And now,' he uncoiled himself and stood up, 'I really must go—can't keep the judge waiting.'

He turned and began to walk purposefully away, leaving Catherine staring after him. Surely he didn't intend to abandon her—he couldn't! She caught him up at the curve of the beach where she saw his own boat pulled up.

'Look,' she demanded, 'you've had your joke—now give me back my plug or—or you'll have to give me a lift. *I* have to get back to town as well as you, you know I do.' She just managed to suppress the incipient wail.

The hull of the boat grated on the sand.

'Sorry to disappoint you, Tiger,' he said over his shoulder, 'but you're going nowhere. Oh, and don't think of trying to row back—in case you haven't noticed, your oars seem to have mysteriously gone missing, too!'

Catherine gazed at him open-mouthed. Did he really believe that by keeping her away from the court he would influence the outcome of the hearing? If so, she must quickly disabuse him and then maybe, even now, she could persuade him to take her with him.

'This case, it's—it's purely a matter of law, not of individuals, you know. It certainly won't affect the verdict one way or the other whether I'm there or not.' Her tone was as convincing as she could make it, but her hopes fell as he merely shrugged casually, so she went on, 'You won't stop the hearing by—by kidnapping me. And anyway, it's a very serious crime, to hold me here against my will,' she added, trying to inject a note of menace into her voice.

But he merely grinned at her across the boat and leapt in. 'Oh, don't worry about me. Catnapping's not such a heinous offence!'

'Please take me with you.' She tried pathos, but he only shook his head at her. 'You're m-mad, completely mad!' she hurled at him. 'I just wonder how I didn't see it before. Absolutely crazy!'

The corners of her mouth turned down and a desperate tear ran down her nose. Uncle Bob would think she had let him down, and Aunt Lu would be worried sick. Luke leaned over and wiped the tear away.

'Oh, Tiger, don't look like that. And don't worry—I'll be back.'

'That's exactly what *is* worrying me!' she shouted at him as he pulled on the starter cord, but he only laughed. The boat gathered itself, burst into life and shot away, leaving a V of white foam in its wake, as Catherine, viciously kicking up the sand to relieve her feelings, turned away and went in search of something to hook down her bikini.

It was early evening before she saw the boat. She hesitated, then swallowed her pride and went down to the water's edge as Luke dragged it on to the sand. He had changed from his shorts into pale blue jeans and a long-sleeved white sweat shirt. Catherine, who had spent a miserable afternoon, alternately sitting on the beach, staring across the two miles of water which separated her from Port Charlotte, pacing round the island and, latterly, fighting off sand flies as evening fell, now felt thoroughly bad tempered.

As Luke leaped lithely ashore, she said sarcastically, 'You've got your best going *court*ing clothes on, I see.'

'My, my—the fresh air has certainly sharpened your

rapier wit,' he drawled. 'But no, these are my overnight clothes. It gets rather chilly at three a.m.'

She gaped at him, the brilliant orange light from the setting sun reflecting directly on their faces—he, perfectly relaxed, she thought, with spurting anger, while she was almost crackling with nervous irritation.

'But—but you're not staying here all night, are you?'

'Well, I suppose I needn't. I just thought you'd be nervous on your own——'

'But I'm not staying here either,' Catherine burst out. 'I *can't*! You've got to take me home!'

He straightened up from where he had been bending over the boat. 'Catch,' he said, and tossed a bundle at her.

With a sinking heart, she saw that it was a blanket and a sleeping-bag and drew herself up with all the dignity she could muster. 'Look, if it's money——'

But he only laughed, and dumped a box on the sand beside her. 'You know,' he said, 'I've told you before, you really must stop thinking all you have to do is wave a fat roll of notes under my nose.'

This time, however, there was no anger in his voice. Only, she thought, with a sudden panic, a bubbling triumph—and she knew, with cold certainty, that against all the odds, he had won the hearing. But in that case, what on earth could he possibly be up to this time? Surely, even he must see that there was no point in prolonging this—this charade a minute longer. There was just no reason for him to force her to stay out here with him all night. Unless—her heart missed a beat, then steadied. No, that was impossible—he had made it abundantly clear that, far from being attracted to her, he regarded her only at best with ironic amusement, but more frequently with open dislike. Perhaps it was simply that he was being his usual cussed self, deliberately engineering things to go his way, for no better reason than that that was what he wanted. Her tired brain gave up the pointless struggle to comprehend his intricate personality.

'Oh, and by the way,' he said, seemingly unconsciously confirming her thoughts, 'the judge dismissed the case of Latham and Hartley versus Devinish. He didn't seem to like the idea of that uncle of yours trying to get the law altered to suit himself—and he wasn't too pleased with the two of you ganging up on a harmless beachcomber.'

'You—harmless!' Sick at heart and regardless of him, she turned away and slumped down heavily on the sand.

Luke came and dropped down beside her. He wrapped an arm casually round her shoulders, but she flinched away from him.

'Listen to me,' he said. 'You're just another mercenary little money-grubber, I know, but—don't look like that. I promise you, things will go better for you very soon. Trust Uncle Luke.'

She wrenched herself free from the disturbing touch of his bare arm against her neck and stood up. 'Trust you!' she said bitterly. 'Not in a million years.'

He shrugged coolly. 'OK, honey—but one way or another, you're staying here tonight, and I'm not open to discussion on that.' He got up, then with a swift look at her, reached across the boat, unhoooked the starter cord, and tucked it in his pocket. 'Just in case you get any crafty ideas in the middle of the night. Now, bring that bedding—we'll go to that old fishermen's refuge.'

So he had been here before, Catherine thought. Maybe he had had this whole crazy scheme planned for some time . . . He lifted out another box from the boat, placed a hurricane lamp on top and, carrying both, walked off, leaving her to follow.

The fishermen's hut was a tiny wooden shack, set well back from the beach among the lush undergrowth. Outside, the sky was still faintly light, but once through the doorway there was abrupt darkness, so that she stumbled against him, then backed hastily away, until her shoulders felt the wall. He struck a match and as he lit the lamp, the hut flared eerily into life and the night outside the oblong of doorway seemed all at once much darker.

Catherine, her legs rather weak and trembling, slid down until she was hunched against the wall, her arms round her knees. This isn't happening, she thought. In a moment, I shall wake up, I shall be at Hope's Mill and Mattie will be opening the louvres and asking if I want breakfast out on the——

'Are you going to sit there all night, looking like Lady Macbeth?' Luke was busy unloading one of the boxes and the ground felt cold and damp beneath her. 'I got these patties at the beach bar—come and eat while they're still warm.'

He unwrapped a large paper package and held out a fragrant, golden meat pattie towards her. She longed to tell him to go to hell and take all his patties with him, but her picnic had been a very long time ago, so she took it, just contenting herself with, 'I suppose I should be grateful you don't intend to starve me.'

'Certainly not,' he responded. 'Although from the feel of you when you landed on top of me out on the beach, well——' He shrugged expressively.

Catherine, refusing to rise to his bait, set her teeth and went on eating in silence. As she ate, she was thinking, So he's won. It's all over . . . no sale, no Coral Strand hotel, no money for the hospital, no money for Uncle Bob. Uncle Bob! She bit her lip hard as she thought of how he must be feeling—and Aunt Lu too. They would be so worried.

'What's the matter now?' From the shadows at the far side of the hut, Luke spoke.

'Oh, nothing—at least, nothing that would bother you.' She blinked the tears away. 'I was just thinking of my uncle and aunt—they'll be out of their minds when I don't go home.' In spite of herself, her voice rose miserably.

'Which is precisely why I dropped that letter from you in at his office this afternoon.'

'Letter? What letter?'

'Oh, you know. Highly apologetic, but called away urgently.'

'You don't expect them to fall for that, surely,' Catherine said scornfully. 'They know my writing too well.'

'Oh, didn't I tell you? Beachcombing isn't my only attribute. I'm a skilled forger as well—although I admit your scrawl took some doing.'

He dug in his pocket and fished out a crumpled piece of paper which he tosssed across to her. She smoothed out the creases and saw that it was a sheet of file paper, covered closely in her large, sprawling hand. She recognised it as a page from one of her old tutorial essays, which she had been using as a bookmark that afternoon in Aunt Lu's garden.

'How did—you stole it!' She scowled at him accusingly then, at the memory of that afternoon, hastily looked away, as unwelcome sensations rose in her.

As though quite unaware of those feelings, Luke said casually, 'Oh, and by the way—there's no need to blame yourself—or me. I'm certain the fact that you weren't in court didn't sway the judge in my favour. Although the way Latham was carrying on outside the court, you'd have thought it was a matter of life and death at the very least.' He smiled reminiscently, then yawned and stretched. 'Well, it's been quite a day. I'm for bed.'

He stood up and shook out the folded sleeping-bag. 'It's a double bag,' he remarked conversationally, 'so we'll manage all right. I promise I don't kick—at least, none of my sleeping partners has ever complained.' He was deftly tucking in the blanket around the bag, not looking at her, as she sprang to her feet in horror.

'But I can't sleep with you!'

Luke gave her a slanting look from under his dark brows and she blushed furiously. 'You know perfectly well what I mean,' she went on angrily, and not all the anger was directed at him. For a moment, the unwanted, *forbidden* picture of herself in his arms had flashed into her mind. 'I cannot share a sleeping-bag with you,' she enunciated very clearly. 'So, in that case, you'll have to sleep somewhere else.'

She bent down and put her hand firmly on the bag.

'Uh, uh—sorry to disappoint you again.' Luke shook his head and his eyes were gleaming in the light from the lamp. 'At thirty-six I'm *much* too old to risk rheumatics from sleeping on damp ground. And, anyway, I'm only just getting over denghi fever—or have you forgotten?' He coughed pathetically.

Catherine stared down at him, completely nonplussed. She darted a glance towards the open door. Beyond the flickering semi-circle of pale golden light which illuminated the nearest bushes and tree-trunks, the blackness was intense, total. She swallowed. Anything could be out there, anything . . . She looked back at Luke, hoping to awaken his chivalry, but at his obvious, open enjoyment of the situation he had created, she made up her mind. Whatever was out there must surely be preferable to a night in this hut. She picked up the blanket and turned to go.

'I hope you won't begrudge me this,' she said coldly.

'And where are you off to?' His voice was amused, even indulgent.

'I'm—I'm going to sleep in my boat. Any objections?'

'Well, watch out for land crabs then. I saw some burrows on the beach.'

Land crabs! Catherine gave an involuntary shudder, but then he went on, 'Still, Tiger Hartley will be more than a match for them, I'm sure.'

So she choked down her fear and, with a last freezing

look, marched out of the hut.

The bottom of the boat was extremely hard and unyielding, but by dint of using the blanket folded and covering herself with her beach towel, Catherine felt reasonably comfortable. Fortunately, the night air was still and she could feel radiated warmth rising gently from the sand. In the bushes close by something rustled. A mouse, or a small bird, she told herself stoutly, and anyway, she was quite safe in the boat.

Around her, the sea moved in slow, dark wrinkles. She lay on her back and, above her, as in an immense bowl of midnight-blue velvet, a full coppery moon and every star in the galaxy shimmered. The sight was deeply reassuring and for the first time that day she felt herself begin to unwind, as though, like the cat that Luke had named her, a giant hand were stroking, smoothing her ruffled fur.

She was all but asleep when she heard the sound; a faint, almost stealthy shuffling. Her eyes flew open and, for a moment, she had no idea where she was. Then, above her head, the hard outline of her boat, darker against the dark sky, reminded her that she was a prisoner. The sound came again, soft, furtive—almost more of a movement than a sound—and she lay still, her heart pounding against her ribs.

The noise came once more, but hurried, urgent, this time. She sat bolt upright and looked over the side of the boat. The moon was obscured by a bank of cloud but the sand still showed up pale, almost phosphorescent, and against it Catherine, with a sick lurch of her stomach, saw shapes—dozens of shapes—moving, scuttling away, then stopping. Her skin crawled at the sight and she swallowed hard, desperately fighting down her irrational fear. The pale, sinister blurs seemed to hesitate then advanced again towards the boat, the obscene, skull-like shapes moving almost soundlessly, the huge white feelers beckoning to her.

Her forehead was wet with sweat and she wiped it

shakily, as strange, childish images contorted her mind.
'Pull yourself together, for Heaven's sake,' she told
herself fiercely. 'You're bigger than they are!' Hearing
her own voice, she realised that she had spoken aloud but
at least the words put some courage into her. She was
about to slide down under the beach towel again, when
there was a sharp, rasping sound against the side of the
boat, under her very hand, it seemed. She eased herself
up again, and, her heart beating erratically, she peered
over the edge. Right below her was an enormous crab, its
feelers still scraping insistently against the side of the
boat, as though hungrily seeking a foothold.

Oh God, it was trying to climb into the boat! Catherine
stared at it in stark terror, then closed her eyes tight. She
put her hands up to her mouth and screamed, again and
again, the screams pealing in her ears. Even when she
felt herself being lifted out of the boat the screams went
on, as though they were coming from someone else, until
they slowly turned to gasping sobs. In the hut, Luke
dropped down on to a packing case and held her, until
the racking spasms began to quieten, then he shook her
lightly.

'Hey, that's enough.' His voice was quite amazingly
gentle. 'The hairs on my chest aren't waterproof. I don't
want them shrinking.'

Catherine's last sobs dissolved into a watery sniffle
and she slowly sat up, brushing at her wet cheeks. 'I'm
sorry.' She spoke to the darkness. Luke was invisible,
only his arms around her and his warm breath against
her face. 'It's just that they were so horrible. I was
frightened.'

'They aren't too pleasant, are they—like something out
of a horror movie.'

'Yes, but it's more than that.' She felt she must make
him understand. 'You see, it reminded me of when I was
a little girl.' She shuddered. 'I suppose I was only about
six. I remember our first house, at school, was wooden,

built up off the ground, and—and land crabs lived underneath. I used to lie in bed sometimes, hearing them . . . Then one night, I couldn't sleep . . . I went out on to the porch. I saw the houseboy . . . he had a torch, and he was shining it down on to some crabs . . . They looked huge and white. Then I saw that he had a machete . . . He lifted it, and began to split the crabs right in two . . . They were still waving their feelers . . . Then I started screaming, and Mum and Dad came rushing out.' She shuddered again. 'I suppose something clicked in my brain tonight, and it all came back.'

She stood up and heard him stand as well. His fingers brushed across her shoulder. 'You'd better use the sleeping-bag.'

'Oh, no—I'll be all right now.' She was suddenly in a hurry to get away. Even the crabs seemed to have lost their menacing quality.

'No, you won't.' His hand tightened on her arm as she shied away. 'You're cold—much too cold to go back out there.' She heard him peel off his sweat shirt and he put it into her hands. 'Put this on.' Then, as she hesitated, he added firmly, 'Do as I tell you.'

As she pulled it over her head, she said, 'It's the rainy season coming on.' Her voice was husky, she didn't seem able to breathe easily and she babbled on, 'It's—it's always like this—very hot and humid, then it turns chilly and the wind gets up.'

As if in answer, the rickety door creaked softly and she went on, 'The rains will start soon—tomorrow, I should think.'

'All the more reason to have you safe in here.' The pressure of his hand was firm, drawing her down, until she dropped on to the sleeping-bag. 'No more arguments—get in. Goodnight—sleep well, Tiger.'

'But—where are you going to sleep?'

She heard him turn and saw his dark bulk in the

doorway, outlined against the night. 'In the boat, of course.'

'No.' Catherine spoke more emphatically than she had intended. 'I—I mean, it's very uncomfortable,' she added lamely, not daring to ask herself why she had not let him go, why she had suddenly felt this need for him to be near her.

'All right, I'll stay here.' His voice was off-hand. 'I'll fetch the blanket.'

Catherine wriggled down into the bag, feeling the residue of warmth from Luke's body enfold her, then she heard him return, spread the blanket and lie down at the far side of the hut.

'Goodnight,' he said.

'Oh—goodnight.'

She turned over and, closing her eyes, tried to shut out her awareness of him, just a few feet away in the darkness. An hour later, as she stared unseeingly up at the roof of the hut, she heard him yet again tossing restlessly to and fro.

'Luke—are you awake?' she whispered, just managing to stifle the nervous giggle that was welling up inside her.

'You bet. God, this floor's even harder than I thought. I think I'll wrap myself in the blanket and try sitting up outside.'

She heard him get to his feet. Good, she thought, serves you right if you have a sleepless night! But then she heard her voice, seemingly speaking of its own volition.

'No—no, it's impossible. You won't sleep. Look—if you like——' terror at her own temerity made her croak '—if you like, there's plenty of room in here.'

'Well—if you're quite sure,' Luke said slowly.

I'm not sure, not at all sure, she thought in panic, but it was too late.

'That's fine, then.' His voice was brisk and a moment later she felt his hands on the top of the bag.

'It's just—well——' she began, and he gave a throaty chuckle.

'Having cold feet so soon? Or just worried that I shall immediately reveal myself as the ravening sex maniac you've always suspected me of being?'

She felt his lean body sliding down beside her and she immediately edged to the farther side of the bag, as though endeavouring to shrink right into the very seams.

'Don't worry, Tiger.' His voice was right at her ear. 'Don't be afraid of me. After all, it's not the first time you've shared a bed with me—and no harm came to you on that occasion. I promise you, all I'm capable of right now is sleep.'

He rolled away from her and, incredulously, she felt his body immediately relax and his breathing become regular and easy. Well! She felt almost deflated. I needn't have worried. A small, secret laugh welled up inside her, and she went to sleep, the smile still lingering on her lips.

CHAPTER SEVEN

CATHERINE woke early, feeling the hard ground against her side. She rolled over on to her back and came up against Luke's unyielding body. Jerking away from the contact, she turned to look at him. In the pre-dawn greyness she could just make out that he was awake and watching her, one hand beneath his head. His eyes looked sombre, reflecting the grey from the doorway. All at once, she panicked and turned her head away.

I must have been mad, utterly mad, she thought. It was the rains—people sometimes did do peculiar, not to say crazy, things before the rains broke. *Why* had she done it? Surely, he had deserved no better than a sleepless night in the boat—and surely she should have been happy to find his bones picked clean this morning by a horde of voracious crabs. No. She swallowed hard. She had got him to stay—invited him into the sleeping-bag, because she——

Her muscles tensed as she gathered herself to plunge out of the bag, but Luke said quietly, 'Don't get up yet, Catherine. I've got something to tell you.'

Catherine? Not Cat—not Tiger?

'I'm leaving—today.'

'L-leaving? What do you mean? You're not going to leave me here on the island again?' Her voice was sharp with panic.

'I'm leaving Coral Strand, leaving Port Charlotte, leaving St Hilaire.' His voice was brusque, almost harsh.

'But you can't be. I don't believe you.'

'I'll show you my plane ticket if you like. One-way ticket, St Hilaire to Heathrow, via New York.'

'You've *bought* a plane ticket.' She spoke slowly,

111

unable to keep the incredulity out of her voice.

'Yes.'

She stared at the dingy matchwood ceiling, quite unable to digest this latest bombshell. Luke leaving? Today?

'Well—go on, then.' His voice was dry. 'Start doing cartwheels round the hut. After all, you've been telling me for weeks that that's what I ought to do.'

'I don't believe you,' she repeated flatly. 'You're fooling with me again—you're good at that, remember?' There was a flicker of anger in her voice now.

'Uh, uh. Scout's honour.'

'B-but why?'

'Well—let's just say, I've won my point of principle—stuck it out in the teeth of all the bribery, blandishments, insults, threats from you and your uncle. So now—I can go.'

'Yes, you can go now.' A surge of bitterness broke into her voice. 'Now that you've ruined everything. You're a sadist, do you know that?' Impervious to his close proximity, she rolled to face him, their eyes inches apart. 'You—you've just stayed long enough to mess us all around, haven't you—Uncle Bob, me, the court. No doubt it's given you great pleasure.'

'Well, if you're going to react like that, maybe I'll change my mind—postpone my trip for a few months.' There was anger stirring in his voice now.

Unable to lie still a moment longer, Catherine hauled herself out of the bag and stumbled from the hut. She felt an overwhelming need to be alone, to think through all the implications of what Luke had just told her, without feeling his sardonic eyes on her, reading her every thought. Oblivious of the brambles clawing at her limbs, she pushed her way through the bushes to her boat, still beached on the shore, and sat down on it. In the half-light, she saw Luke's footprints, deep and hurried, where he had run to her. They blurred suddenly and danced in

front of her eyes, until she blinked hard and turned to
watch the sun as it slowly surged above the horizon,
turning the sea in an instant from grey to a sheen of
opalescence.

Two miles away, the rays lit the waterfront wharves
and the hills behind Port Charlotte. She fancied she
could even see Cinnamon House, perched on its ridge.
Cinnamon House ... Uncle Bob ... he'd be wild with
delight at her news, she thought dully—for she did not
any longer doubt Luke's words. And she also was—wild
with delight. It didn't matter in the least now that the
court had found against them. The obstacle in the way of
the sale of Coral Strand had suddenly, inexplicably, been
removed—had removed himself—and there was nothing
in the world now to prevent the deal with Brannan
International from going ahead ...

And yet, try as she would to fix in her mind the correct
picture—Coral Strand sold, she and her uncle triumphant—another image kept sliding across, obscuring
that one: Luke's face, which soon she would never see
again. How could she bear it? Her face puckered, as a
feeling of such desolate emptiness welled up from the
lowest depths of her being, that momentarily she closed
her eyes, then ramming her hands into the pouch of
Luke's sweatshirt, she stared out to sea.

Once and for all, she told herself sternly, *will* you pull
yourself together? What's wrong with you, anyway? For
someone who's *supposed* to be intelligent, you're being
completely stupid. So snap out of it. He's going—for
good. Great, marvellous. Best news for years. Having
said which, aloud, to a tiny sand-bug which was busy
stalking her feet, she stood up and walked slowly back to
the hut.

The early morning light was brilliant now, but when
she ducked through the low doorway the interior was like
a warm, black hole. Luke was not there. She would get
her bag, the one which, an eternity ago, she had packed

at Hope's Mill, and——

'Catherine?'

Startled, she turned to see Luke standing in the doorway. She put her hands up, not knowing whether she was shielding herself from him or reaching out to him, but he seemed unaware of her action.

'I was just going to get breakfast.'

Breakfast? She stared at him. After calmly telling her that all the turmoil, the violence even, of their forced relationship was over—breakfast?

'Oh, don't bother for me—I'm not hungry.' Somehow, she made her voice as flat and expressionless as his.

As though reluctant, he came slowly across to her. 'You should eat something. I don't want you feeling seasick when we go back.'

'Hardly. It's only two miles.' She attempted a careless laugh, but the sound that came was a pathetic travesty. 'I—I'll get my things.'

She took a step away, then caught her foot in the sleeping-bag. Before she could even gasp, Luke's hands came up in a lightning reflex action and steadied her. At that same moment, the rays of the sun burst full into the hut and they looked at each other as though for the very first time, their faces gilded, a halo of brilliance around their hair. For a long, long moment they looked, as if devouring each other's faces, and Catherine felt an almost tangible current of electricity leap from Luke's body, through his fingers, resting lightly on her arms, and into her.

In the harsh sunlight, tiny motes of dust danced round the sleazy hut, but they stood quite motionless, hardly breathing, as though held in a golden web. Then she felt his hands slowly, so slowly, almost unwillingly, drawing her to him, until his warm breath stirred the wisps of hair at her temples. Then, still slowly, his lips came down, brushing softly across hers in the most delicate of kisses. He raised his head for an instant, then kissed her again.

He pressed her to him and she felt a fierce hunger in his lips. She responded to it with a hunger of her own, locking her hands in the thick dark hair to draw him even closer. He slid his mouth across her cheek, her skin taking fire under his lips, then he buried his face in her throat.

'Oh, Catherine, Catherine—I want you.'

His muffled voice was harsh, almost angry. She felt his hands under the sweatshirt, moving against her hot skin, and she shivered with sweet pleasure. Somewhere, far at the back of her mind, a cold, clear voice was saying, this is madness, but a crazy recklessness swept through her, drowning everything in the need to have Luke hold her, love her, *love* her.

She leaned against him for support and, locked in the circle of each other's arms, they slowly crumpled to the floor. His hands pulled aside the sweatshirt and warm skin met warm skin. Catherine shuddered against him. 'Oh, Luke . . .' It was a sigh.

He raised his head and looked at her. How could she ever have thought that face arrogant, those grey eyes hostile? She smiled up at him, a drowning, tremulous smile, and in that same instant his face changed, shifted before her eyes, into the old hard, unyielding lines. As she stared at him, he jerked away from her.

'Cover yourself up.'

'W-what?' She still stared up at him.

'I said cover yourself up.'

The old harshness was back too, and her eyes stung for a moment, until she bit viciously on her lower lip. Slowly, stiffly, she sat up and carefully, with hands that fumbled slightly, she hooked up her bikini top then, with a convulsive movement, as though unable to bear its touch against her skin a moment longer, she tore off his sweatshirt and threw it on to the ground between them. Somewhere inside her, beneath the shock and the—yes, grief, stirred her old shame and anger. She shot him one quick glance as he sat hunched on the floor, staring out of the doorway, seemingly oblivious of her presence. Then, with an obvious effort, he spoke.

'I'm sorry, Catherine.' His voice was remote, and he still stared out, as though at some far away darkness.

He felt for her hand, and held it. At the touch of his palm against hers, a faint, involuntary desire flickered inside her, but then sick outrage swept this aside. She dragged her hand from his, as his words echoed hollowly in her brain.

'Why should you be?' Her voice was shaking. 'I mean—you got the—the desired reaction yet again, didn't you?'

'Stop it, Catherine.' His dark brows were drawn down in an angry frown.

'Why should I? It's true.' For heaven's sake, would her voice never stop shaking? Yet again, he had tried—and yet again, he had succeeded. She dug her nails into her palms. He thought she was just a little tramp and, after all, any outsider looking on would have been excused for a shrug, a deprecating smile, as she tried to protest her innocence. She swallowed hard.

'And I suppose you'll be able to boast—to your—what's the word?' Her voice was pitched high. 'Your cronies.'

'Catherine, stop it.' Luke looked really angry now. He seized her hand and shook it in emphasis. 'Listen to me. It wasn't like that this time, I swear.'

'You—*swear*!' she burst out. She wanted to lash out, hurt him, as he had shamed and hurt her.

'Yes—on my honour.'

He held her gaze and something intangible, almost a sternness, kept her silent. He loosed his grip on her hand and began gently stroking his thumb across her palm.

'You're very beautiful, Catherine—like a ripe, sun-warmed peach. I don't think you realise quite the effect you have on susceptible males.' He smiled at her rather wryly, and something in his eyes made her drop hers in confusion as her heart skipped unsteadily. 'And more than that—you have a kind of joyous vitality, which reaches out to others.'

He put his arm round her shoulders and gently pulled her towards him until she was leaning against him, but this time, as the last of her anger and shame evaporated, there was only a delicious sense of easy rightness at feeling her bare skin against him. He rubbed his face gently against her head, his stubbly chin catching the soft tendrils around her hairline.

'You need a shave,' she said, putting up her hand and shyly caressing his cheek.

It was as though she were still holding her breath, she thought involuntarily, afraid that this gilded, fragile circle of intimacy that enclosed them both would burst, like a child's soap-sud bubble.

He laughed against her hair. 'Drifters never shave, you know that.' He sniffed. 'Mmm, your hair smells delicious—like the cowslips and lady's smock in the hay meadows outside Curlieus.'

'Curlieus?'

'My home—in England.' There was an almost imperceptible change in his voice, but Catherine, feeling an overwhelming need to learn about this man, persisted.

'Curlieus,' she said the word slowly, 'that's an unusual name for a house.'

'Yes,' he agreed, 'I suppose it is. I've never really thought about it. As far as I know it's been Curlieus since the day it was built over two hundred years ago.'

She risked another question, even though she felt as though she were treading on eggs. 'Where is your house?'

'In Norfolk, near the sea and the salt marshes.'

'Mmm, it sounds lovely,' Catherine murmured, but he laughed.

'I doubt whether *you*'d think so. The wind comes

straight in from Siberia—it would soon finish off a sun-loving type like you.' She thought she detected, momentarily, a faintly bitter inflection in his tone but then, after a pause, he added, 'But I love it.'

There was no mistaking now the unconscious longing in his tone and she steeled herself to ask the question she knew she had to ask.

'And do you live there on your own?'

She felt his arm stiffen for a moment and there was another pause.

'You ask too many questions. Remember—curiosity killed the cat!'

He spoke mildly enough, but Catherine sensed the implicit warning and she knew that it would be futile, if not dangerous, to try to probe any further. But at least her persistence had broken the golden spell that was threatening to entwine them, and this was all to the good. She had to get back to Port Charlotte, to Uncle Bob's office, in time to tell the Brannan representatives that Luke was leaving.

'I'll get us some breakfast,' she said, 'and then I must go.'

But even as she went to move, he uncoiled himself, catlike, and went and leaned against the doorpost.

'Sorry, Catherine, but you aren't going anywhere—at least, not this morning.'

She stared at him in puzzlement, at first unable to comprehend quite what he was saying.

'B-But you don't understand. I *must* go, Luke. I've got to get back to town. I have to—that is, Uncle Bob and Lu will be so worried about me.'

'Well, they'll just have to worry for a while longer.' She flinched at the old curt decisiveness, back in his voice. 'I've told you—you're not going.'

She sprang to her feet and confronted him, hands on hips. Yet again, she had been deceived. That golden bubble of joyous intimacy had been an illusion, she thought miserably, and the knowledge gave a cutting edge to her anger.

'And I'm telling you, Luke Devinish, I must go, I *will* go.'

He gave her a cold look. 'For the last time, you're not—at least, not until I choose to let you go.'

He left the doorway and began sorting through the food box then, as Catherine watched in baffled rage, he threw out, 'If you want to eat, come and help.'

'No, I won't, damn you.'

He glanced up at her briefly, then turned his attention back to the food. 'I gave you your chance yesterday,' he said, 'and you refused to take it. And that's why, Cat, you will not be at your uncle's office this morning, either to tell him the good news about my plane ticket, or to sign any contract with Ritter.'

'Ritter?' she asked wanly.

'The Brannan representative—who else?'

Her heart plummeted. So all her hopes had been futile. He did know about the meeting—knew even more about it than she did, it seemed. Even now she had managed to underestimate him. Was there anything about this whole wretched business that he did not know? Almost certainly not, she told herself grimly. So it was nothing to do with the court hearing—or, at least, that was merely incidental—why she had been first marooned, then imprisoned here, and not only that—she could see only too clearly that Luke was fully determined to continue her enforced captivity for exactly as long as it would take to thwart Brannan—and herself—to the last.

Another frightening thought struck her. He would be leaving the cay some time that day. Would he not even release her then? Did he—her mouth went dry—did he intend to leave her here alone, with no one knowing where she was, while he sailed off to catch his flight? Impossible, she told herself stoutly. Even Luke Devinish could not be so ruthless. And yet . . . Well, she would face that if and when it happened. In the meantime, she didn't have to stay here meekly within reach of his taunting gaze. She could at least ensure that he enjoyed his triumph alone.

'Let me know when you're graciously prepared to let me go,' she said, ice crackling in her voice. 'Until then— well, let's just say I'd rather not set eyes on you.'

She retreated to the far end of the cay, to spend a solitary morning, not swimming, just hunched gloomily on a small spit of sand, looking across to the mainland, elusive and tantalising.

Finally, she heard Luke calling to her and when she got back he was bending over her boat, just replacing the plug. As she approached, hiding her feeling of relief, he pushed the boat into shallow water and tossed in the oars, which were lying on the sand. Without even a glance in his direction, she threw her gear into the well of the boat, pushed it further out and scrambled in. With her back to him, she pulled the starter cord and the engine coughed then fired into life.

'Goodbye, Cat.'

She heard his voice above the throb of the engine but she wasn't going to look, wasn't even going to acknowledge his presence . . . Fifty yards off-shore, she darted one quick look over her shoulder. Luke was standing at the water's edge and when he saw her he gave a wave which, even at that distance, managed to be ironic. Then he turned, walked swiftly across the beach, and was lost among the bushes.

Goodbye, Luke Devinish. She would never see him again, and she was glad.

During the morning, the weather had turned overcast and as she approached the mainland Catherine had a good view of the wicked black storm clouds, already piled over the inland hills and rolling slowly down towards the town. By the time she arrived at Bob

Latham's office there were heavy splats of rain across the windscreen and she heard the first low, menacing growl of thunder.

How could she face Uncle Bob? Catherine swallowed nervously and paused for a moment, her hand on the door-knob, to brace herself for his amazed and no doubt at first reproachful, even angry, exclamations, then took a deep breath and plunged into the room. But it was Catherine herself who was completely taken aback. He was just in the act of clinking champagne glasses with two West Indian men in well cut, pale grey business suits.

'Good lord, Catherine! Where on earth have you been? But it doesn't matter now—you're just the girl we need.' As she gaped at him, he went on, 'Cathy, meet Steve Bennet and Errol King.' He grinned at her. 'They've just put in an offer for Coral Strand—a very fair offer, although of course, as they no doubt appreciate, they have a bargain.'

He slopped a generous measure of champagne into a glass and thrust it at her. Light began to dawn on Catherine and she smiled broadly. 'So Brannan have decided to buy after all——'

But Bob Latham clapped her on the shoulder jovially. 'Brannan? Who said anything about Brannan? No— they've withdrawn, and good riddance to them. Ritter rang me this morning to say they've clinched a sale on St Jago Island—must have had it all lined up, just in case things didn't work out for us in court yesterday.' He beamed at the two men. 'Glad of it—no time for these faceless, multinational companies. Give me your home-grown West Indian company any time.'

'Hmm.' There was more than a hint of ironic amusement in Errol King's voice. 'And yet you know, Bob, the last time we were in touch with you we had the distinct impression that you didn't quite believe we'd really be able to get our act together and you much preferred to do a deal with Brannan.'

Catherine stared at him ... We were in touch with you ...? Preferred to do a deal with Brannan ...? Realisation hit her, almost like a physical blow, and she started momentarily, so that some of the champagne spilt over the rim, trickling down her fingers in icy droplets. So there *was* another group, had been all along. Luke had been telling the truth—it was Uncle Bob who had lied to her! Anger flared in her and she turned accusing eyes on him. He caught her scorching gaze and had the grace to look abashed, almost guilty for an instant. Then he spread his hands in a deprecating gesture.

'Sorry, love. I know I should have told you, but at the time—well, all right, I admit it. Brannan, with an open cheque book and unlimited resources *did* seem a better proposition than a local group who I knew, behind the scenes, were having serious problems raising enough money.'

'Well, yes,' agreed Bennet, 'we can tell you now that we were having a few financial difficulties. So you see, Miss Hartley,' he gave Catherine a keen look in which there was more than a hint of private amusement, 'that's why we needed your squatter.'

She gaped at him. 'So you mean Luke—the squatter— parking himself on my land—it was a set-up right from the start!'

Steve Bennet laughed and spread his hands deprecatingly. 'It was unpardonable, I know, Miss Hartley—and Luke was truly sorry about it——' oh, yes, like hell he was, thought Catherine '—but it was the only way we could think of to keep Brannan at bay. You see, Luke and I are old friends, from Oxford and law-school days——'

Catherine stared at him, her eyes widening. Oxford! Law-school! Well, at least she had been right about Luke on that score—about the only thing about him that she had got right, she thought bitterly.

'But I still don't understand.' She wrinkled her forehead in puzzlement. 'How did he get involved?'

'Well, he was—rather at a loose end. There have been some—er—family troubles at home. He had to come across to Miami to sort one or two things out——' Catherine caught the faintly cautious inflection of the habitual lawyer '—and from there he came on down to see me in Barbados. I was in the thick of trying to raise the last of the capital to counter the Brannan bid. He decided against coming in with us financially, unfortunately. Oh, yes,' as he saw her expression, 'Luke is a very wealthy man—but he did agree to take the part of squatter-in-residence. He was always keen on acting when we were up at Oxford—and I gather he made quite a success of the role, eh, Miss Hartley?'

Catherine smiled politely but inwardly she was seething. Yes, she thought, and didn't he just enjoy every minute of it!

'Things were reaching a head this week, but it was touch and go whether we could finalise our offer in time. If the case had gone against Luke—and privately he wasn't at all confident that it wouldn't—well,' he shrugged, 'the deal with Brannan could have been signed and sealed under our very noses. So we asked Luke to try and win us another twenty-four hours, which is why he decided to take—er, drastic measures. I gather that he was still trying to work out what to do when you played right into his hands. He spotted you sailing off to that cay, followed you and—well, *persuaded* you to stay until today.'

'Good lord!' Uncle Bob burst in. 'Are you saying he *kidnapped* her? So that's what you meant when you assured me that she would be back today. Well, well— the young devil!'

He laughed uproariously but Catherine regarded him stonily. Well, he always has had an unpredictable sense of humour, she thought sourly.

'Anyway,' he went on, still smiling broadly, 'you ought to be grateful to Luke, love. Steve here is more than

happy to give us the safeguards you were always on at me
to try to tear out of Brannan—local materials, low-level
building, all that sort of thing, and——'

'So I'm sure, Miss Hartley,' Bennet interrupted, 'in
time you'll find it in your heart to forgive us—and Luke.'

Catherine thrust her bunched fists into the pockets of
her shorts. Forgive him? She had been kidnapped, used,
manipulated—God, how she had been manipulated,
from square one onwards!

'I'll do my best,' she said, somehow forcing a cool
smile.

There was an awkward pause—Catherine trying hard
not to glower at the entire room, and Bob looking as
though he was not quite sure what all the undercurrents
were about. He snatched up the bottle gratefully. 'More
champagne?'

'Oh, no, thanks.' Bennet shot back his white cuff.
'We'd better be moving. Luke's plane leaves at six, and
we're meeting him before he goes. I expect he's cleaning
out that disreputable hut of his.'

They shook hands, amid promises that the draft
documents would be prepared the next day, and under
cover of their departure Catherine put down her
untouched champagne and sidled towards the door. She
too needed to get away, to escape Uncle Bob's apologies,
exclamations, questions, triumph.

CHAPTER EIGHT

As HE waved the men off in their chauffeured limousine, she said hastily, "Bye, Uncle Bob—I'll see you later.'

As she spoke, there was a flash of lightning and the skies opened. Not giving him time to reply, she ran down the street to her car and flung herself in, already soaked to the skin.

The steep, rutted road up to Hope's Mill was awash with water, so that by the time she turned off on to her drive, the car was almost aqua-planing. There was no sign of Mattie—Catherine realised, with relief, that as usual when a violent storm was raging she had retreated to bed, her head buried under a couple of pillows and wanting only to be left alone. She showered, then slipped into a cotton housecoat and sat out on the veranda, oblivious of the jagged lightning flickering continually around the hills, and the deep rolls of thunder. She almost welcomed this first, cataclysmic outburst of the rainy season, mirroring as it did her own inner turmoil.

She sat there until the wind veered and the fierce rain drove in across the veranda, forcing her to retreat indoors. She wandered around, then took up a book and tried to read, but the room was dark and when she flicked the switch, the electricity was off. That strange, fidgety restlessness sent her pacing about the house again until, at last, she sat on her bed, chin on knees, and stared raptly at the Paisley-patterned bedspread.

Why hadn't Luke told her, explained . . . ? But he did, a cold inner voice mocked her . . . 'Why won't you even consider selling to anyone else . . . ? That uncle of yours— he must have told you . . .' Or rather, he had tried and she, in her pride and anger, had refused to listen. The anger, though, had burned itself out in a final spurt back in Uncle Bob's office and now, she realised, there was only a listless, dragging feeling ... Oh, God, what *was* the matter with her?

The ticking of the bedside clock roused her from her stupor. Tick-tock, tick-tock—the sound seemed to echo in her brain. Was it ticking faster and faster? Surely not, and yet Catherine felt her heart beating more and more rapidly, as though to keep time. It was reminding her that *now*, at this moment in time—the out-worn cliché was fitting, for once—Luke was still here on St Hilaire, whereas, when the small hand had travelled——

She banged her hands down on her knees and sat bolt upright. Oh, how I wish I'd never owned the wretched beach, she moaned to herself. That way, I would never have met him, never been forced to join battle with him ... Luke, this man who was more than in her mind perpetually—he seemed to have pervaded her blood stream, to be in her very nerve-endings. She closed her eyes to keep out the images, but they crowded against her tightly closed lids; Luke's face, as he lay asleep beside her here, in *this* room ... the island—Luke's face again, but this time coming towards her, his features brilliant in the morning sun, his grey eyes not cold but dark with passion and——

Her eyes shot open as a white flash illuminated the shadowy room. This was it—she recognised the subconscious terror she had thrust far down, the fear that Luke's lovemaking on Mangrove Cay had been like everything else about him, as she now knew—a calculating, coldhearted sham ... She felt a sob rising in her throat and forced it back, biting her lip until she tasted blood. She mustn't begin to cry—she would never stop crying if she once began.

Stiffly, she eased herself up from her cramped position and stood by the window. That intense lightning flash had marked the end of the storm—for that day. The rumbles of thunder were retreating out to sea and the rain was easing, so that already the sweet scents were drifting in from the garden to her on the cool air. It would be a lovely evening. She might even drive down to the nearest beach for a swim—it would do her good. And tomorrow, she would go to Cinnamon House as though nothing had happened . . . then bury herself in hard work. It would not be difficult—the first guests were due in a few days. She was glad that Luke had gone. His disturbing presence had made life altogether too—complicated. Now, well—there was the sale of Coral Strand to be finalised then, at last, her plans for the hospital could be instigated. Working with Aunt Lu would be great fun. She was really looking forward to that . . .

Catherine was surprised to find two huge tears overflowing her eyes and trickling slowly down her cheeks. You little fool, she thought. Everything's going to be just fine now, and you won't be looking over your shoulder all the while to see what *he*'s up to. After all— she managed to smile faintly to herself—that's what you came back here for, wasn't it? To settle down, get yourself some roots, and have a marvellous life. Sunshine, swimming, helping Aunt Lu build up what would obviously soon be a thriving business . . . No, other people could keep their hay meadows and their houses called Curlieus—and their cold winds and grey skies.

She straightened her back and, defiantly singing 'Everything's Coming Up Roses', went along to the kitchen. She didn't really feel at all hungry but, after all, she must eat. The fridge was humming softly—good, the power supply had been restored. Perhaps something hot would be good—some cheese on toast, and soup. Yes, that would be fine. She went into Mattie's dry goods store, peering along the shelves. She reached for a tin of soup then, as if transfixed, stood perfectly still, as the tin of tomato soup slid through her fingers and crashed to the floor. It was one of the tins she had bought on that morning a century ago. Luke ... The misery of that morning, finding him gone, when for a few moments the world had seemed to lurch unsteadily beneath her feet—it all flooded back. And this time, there was no secret consolation to hug to her, no 'Oh well, I'll see him tomorrow'. This time, he was going for ever.

Catherine knew suddenly that she couldn't let Luke go, not like this—without a word, without a smile. Probably he would not want to see her—after all, his job was finished now and she had just been a part of that job, but none the less, she must take the risk of his being off-hand, showing her only the old, unfeeling arrogance. She would just walk up to him, hold out her hand, and say, 'No hard feelings, Luke—and anyway, I'm glad you won.' Then they would shake hands and she would wish him Bon Voyage, and perhaps she might even stay to wave as he walked out across the tarmac ...

She glanced at the kitchen clock. Five o'clock. She had an hour—plenty of time, but still, in her bedroom she found herself tearing impatiently at the ribbons of her housecoat, only to stand indecisively in front of her open wardrobe. Come on, come on, she thought, what the hell does it matter what you wear? But, for some strange, unaccountable reason, it did matter. She pulled out her newest dress, in a fine aquamarine lawn, sleeveless with a low scoop neck and fullish skirt. She dragged it on, then combed out her newly washed hair, so that it hung down in a silky brown mane, then ran to the car ...

The rain had quite stopped now and Port Charlotte was full of people who had retreated indoors during the storm. Cars, donkey-carts, goats, pedestrians—surely, never had it taken so long to negotiate the town. Catherine, fuming with impatience, rounded a bend and braked violently, as just ahead she saw a long line of stationary cars and buses and a policeman waving her down.

He came over to her. 'Sorry, miss, you can't pass. The gully's down.'

The gully! Catherine's stomach leaped with panic, then plummeted down somewhere past her knees.

'B-but I've got to get through to the airport!' she protested and took hold of the gear lever, but the policeman shook his head firmly.

'You can't go, miss. Two cars have been swept out already.'

He left her and as he went back down the patient line, Catherine's hands slumped on the wheel. That gully! she thought fiercely. All her life there'd been talk of bridging the Charlotte River but nothing had been done—after all, people argued, why build a bridge when for three hundred and fifty days in the year the grandly named river was no more than a muddy trickle or a shallow dried up dip in the road? It was only on a handful of occasions that a flash flood on the Heights turned it into a raging torrent, capable of picking up a car—or even on one occasion, she remembered, a whole bus—and depositing it, looking faintly self-conscious, twenty yards out to sea. The Heights—Catherine's heart bounded, as she remembered the track which led, or at least, used to—she hadn't been up there for years—past the Heights, through the hills and down again to come out—surely—yes, near the airport.

She reversed and turned up towards the Heights, along a winding road with a steep drop to one side, but she was unaware of that. Every fibre, every atom in her body was straining towards the airport. Once past the Heights, a select area favoured for its green coolness, the route rose even more steeply and she was forced to abandon all thoughts to the simple necessity of struggling to stay on the muddy track. Her one prayer, over and over again was please, *please* don't let the road have been washed away. She drove through a sleepy shanty town, as hens scattered for their lives and fierce-looking pigs trotted nimbly away, and by the time she began the slow, awkward descent to the coast again, a strange feeling almost of light-headedness gripped her so that when ahead of her she glimpsed the sea, she almost sang aloud for joy.

She raced down the palm-lined drive to the airport and on to the car park. Through the mesh fence she could see the London plane, already arrived from Caracas. It was standing ready on the tarmac, but workmen were still busy round it like ants. She was in time! Snatching up her bag with unsteady fingers, she hurried towards the small, unpretentious terminal building. She pushed open the smoked glass door and went in, her hands clammy on her bag, her eyes searching feverishly. Where was he? There seemed to be no one left in the departure area, except one dark-suited man by the exit door. Surely they couldn't have gone—the passengers from Caracas were still milling about in the arrivals section behind her.

Above her head, the tannoy anounced the departure of the flight for Heathrow via New York. The same panic seized her as back at Hope's Mill. Perhaps Luke hadn't arrived yet. Yes, that would be it—he had been delayed by the rains too. She turned, as though expecting to see him in the car park, then——

'Cathy, honey!'

Nick, suitcase in hand, was in front of her but she looked past him, hardly registering his presence.

'You came to meet me? That's great, Cathy!' Nick's face split into a broad grin of exultation, and before she could answer he had swept her up into his arms. 'Congratulate me, honey. I've just pulled off the business deal of the decade!'

He bent his head and kissed her full on the lips, but she wriggled back from him. 'That's marvellous, Nick, but I must——' Then she was silenced by another kiss.

It was as she jerked back her head, gasping for breath, that she saw Luke, watching her. He had been there all the time, after all—it was just that, in that fleeting, panic-stricken moment, her searching eyes had taken in only a tall, elegant, dark-suited stranger and had flickered past. Well, of course—he was hardly likely to be travelling in shorts and an old T-shirt, was he?

As their eyes met, he gave her one searing look, then, as she hung frozen in Nick's arms, he picked up his attaché case and walked towards the departure door. Hardly conscious of what she was doing, she pulled away from Nick and scrambled under the rope barrier that divided the two areas. Luke was at the door now, he was holding his ticket out to the uniformed girl at the desk. Catherine took a few steps towards him and opened her mouth to call his name, but the word simply would not come. Very deliberately, it seemed, and without another glance at her, he took back his ticket, smiled down at the girl then put his hand on the door. It fell to behind him with a soft thud and she heard his footsteps echoing along the tiled corridor.

Catherine took another step towards the door, then stopped. She realised that she was shivering uncontrollably. This stupid air-conditioning! She wanted to fold up on the ground, right where she was, but she must not do that. No, she must go home. Moving very slowly, as though she had suddenly become an old woman, she turned away. Nick was still there but she couldn't hear what he was saying—she was trapped behind a pane of clear glass and nothing could get through. She made him understand in the end that she didn't want to talk to him—she supposed she must have hurt him, but somehow at this moment it didn't seem to matter.

In the car, she leaned her aching head down on the steering-wheel for a few minutes then looked up, as the plane engines began to rev gently. The doors were closed, all the passengers would be strapped in neatly. If Luke was sitting in a nearside seat he would be able to see her. The plane was only a few yards away—he could be watching her now. She wondered if, at this distance, he would see the anguish that must be written on her face. But she mustn't let him see it—surely she had enough pride for that.

She started the car and, keeping her eyes away from the plane, drove out of the airport. She had thought that once she was away she would feel better, but the stifling misery that had engulfed her was settling on her until she could hardly breathe. She suddenly knew what it was— she had to pass Coral Strand. She faltered, then, as though someone else were in control, she slowed and, as on the day of her arrival just a few short weeks before, she turned off the road. It was, she thought involuntarily, as though Luke, even now, was dragging her towards the only place where she could be near him.

Inside the hut, though, there was nothing of Luke, and Catherine, after a hasty look round, slumped down listlessly on the neatly rolled mattress. The place was so impersonal—it was as though he had deliberately set out to destroy any tangible link with the island. It had been ridiculous for her to come. Luke wasn't here—how could he be? She must never come here again.

As she got up rather awkwardly she saw something lying over in the corner, half hidden behind an upturned packing-case. Slowly, she stooped to retrieve it, turning it over in her hands. It was a small, leather-bound volume and when she glanced at the spine she saw, without surprise, that it was a book of John Donne's love poetry. Inside, there was a gilt printed address label, and someone had written, in a flowing, extravagant scrawl, 'To my darling Luke—all my love, S'.

She was staring down at it stupidly when, in the distance, she heard the roar of engines. Still holding the book in her hands, she stood on Coral Strand and saw Luke's plan, already a tiny silver bird. It was gaining height rapidly and as she watched it turned northwards, leaving a spume of smoke in the still evening air.

She watched with a dreadful intensity until it disappeared then slowly she slid to her knees. One day, she thought, I shall laugh at all this. I shall say to someone I love—There was a man, oh, a long time before you, my darling, and I chased after him to the airport, through flooded roads . . . And then we'll both laugh, and he'll say, You never chased *me* to any airport, and . . .

Catherine tried to smile, but then her composure cracked into fragments, for at last she knew. She loved Luke Devinish—had loved him, in spite of all her angry protestations to herself, almost since the first time she had seen him, here at Coral Strand. She loved him—and he was gone for ever. She crouched on the sand, like a wounded animal, and the bitter tears ran down her face unchecked.

CHAPTER NINE

CATHERINE set down her cup. Outside the coffee-bar, the hotel staff were already busy and she watched idly as they began dismantling the display stands of the Caribbean Calypso, in preparation for the next in-house event, a weekend in Transylvania. Yes, she had to admit Aunt Lu had been right to make her come, against all her protests, to London for this tourist promotion. For the last five months she had hurled herself into work at Cinnamon House and she *had* needed a break. The Caribbean Calypso had turned out to be continuously busy, exhilarating, and finally exhausting, but it had been the change she had craved and she was beginning to feel brighter than she had done for weeks, ready for the winter season.

She had even, she reflected sardonically, become quite an accomplished saleswoman, convincing several people that a mid-winter vacation in St Hilaire, preferably staying at a pleasant spot called Cinnamon House, was just what, unknowingly, they had been waiting for all their lives. How was Mandy making out, she wondered, helping Aunt Lu in her place? She had certainly got a good business head, that girl, and, she had to admit, wasn't afraid of hard work—not that she needed to work now, of course. Catherine smiled to herself.

In the meantime . . . she pursed her lips in thought. The excitement, the flow of adrenalin that had carried her along through the week was slowly faltering and she was beginning to feel ever so slightly deflated. She had said her goodbyes to her new friends, smilingly resisted yet more pressing invitations to 'show her the town' and now, suddenly, it seemed a very long time until her flight early on Monday morning.

She took another sip of coffee. This was ridiculous. Today was Friday—she wasn't going to just moon around until then. There were dozens of things she could do—early Christmas shopping, visit the National Gallery to see her favourite paintings once more ... She could even stay in the hotel for the weekend. She smiled to herself a shade ruefully—even a weekend with Count Dracula would surely be preferable to another three days with Uncle Bob's sister and her family in Hounslow—sharing a bedroom with Debbie, the younger daughter, who was already sullen and pouting because her boyfriend had spent the entire week ogling Catherine ...

Aunt Lu's parting words came involuntarily into her mind: 'Stay on a few days. Look up old acquaintances.' She toyed with the idea of calling on Maggie, her former flat-mate, but somehow that part of her life seemed irrevocably finished ... Well, she couldn't sit here all morning. She dug in her bag for her purse, and her fingers closed on—a slim, leather-bound book. She drew it out slowly and sat very still, oblivious of the bustle around her ...

Old acquaintances ... Luke ... a few hours away from her, almost within her hand's reach ... Of course, that was what she must do. In fact, now that she had finally allowed herself to confront the idea, she acknowledged that she had known it was inevitable, yet had fought against its inevitablity, ever since she had reluctantly agreed to the suggestion that she came to London. With a mixture of trepidation, elation, fear even, she knew that it would be quite impossible for her to leave England without having been to Norfolk.

She would not actually *call* on Luke, of course. Well, he would surely not be pleased to see her—faintly amused perhaps, but not pleased. She closed her eyes momentarily against the pain, as she saw once more his face that last time at the airport . . . All the same, she needed to see the village where he lived, his house—Curlieus—so that she could carry that memory back with her, and perhaps that would finally lay the aching ghost for ever . . .

Less than two hours later, Catherine had loaded her weekend bag into the car, said hurried thanks to Uncle Bob's sister and was looking at the map provided by the car-hire firm. She had no need to check on Luke's address—like Mary Tudor with Calais, she thought with a touch of grim humour, it was engraved indelibly on her heart. Her eyes skimmed feverishly from London to that spot, near the north Norfolk coast, which her mind, in those first heartbroken days, had so often fled to, even as one scratches frantically at an insect bite while knowing it will only make it worse—that tiny dot on the map which spelt sunny hay meadows . . . Curlieus . . . Luke . . .

But, after all, there were no sunny hay fields in evidence late that afternoon. Of course not, she thought. All the hay was gathered in weeks ago, most of the fields had been ploughed into dark ridged corduroy for winter, and the sky was overcast, threatening rain. Meanwhile, the village lay a mile or so ahead. Catherine had turned off the main road several miles back and was driving down a narrow lane, between a deep-cut channel of swirling water and marshy reed-beds. Now—too soon, she thought involuntarily—she could see the squat tower of a church, some red-pantiled roofs among trees. Perhaps one of them was Curlieus, she thought, with a quick, unsteady breath.

There was a film of drizzle on the windscreen and she leaned forward, her attention momentarily diverted from the road ahead as her fingers fumbled among the unfamiliar knobs, so that she missed the warning sign and saw the sharp turn, the narrow dog-leg bridge, an instant too late. There was a loud, jarring noise, which seemed to go on for ever, then a sharp impact. The buckle of her seat belt gave way and she jerked forward, striking her head against the windscreen. The blow knocked her back and she sat quite still for a few moments, staring down stupidly at her hands, which rested limply on the dashboard, and thinking, it was when I stopped for that cup of tea, I can't have fastened the seat belt properly.

Somehow, she forced herself out of the car, on trembling legs, and leaned against it. The vehicle was wedged firmly against the corner stone of the bridge, one front wheel only inches from the sheer drop. The windscreen wipers were working overtime. Well, at least I found the right knob, she thought, and that seemed very funny, so she giggled. The giggle seemed to go on for a long time until, with a tremendous effort, she somehow pulled herself together.

Her teeth were chattering, her hands trembling. She must be cold—yes, that was it. She dragged out her fur jacket and slipped it on, grateful for its comforting warmth. But when she looked around, there was no more comfort, just the fine rain settling on her, the greenish water swirling almost at her feet, and somewhere out among the reeds the harsh cry of a sea bird. Tiny spirals of unease welled up in her, threatening to choke her, to turn into blind panic. She bunched her fists in her jacket pockets and squeezed her eyes tight shut.

Oh, God, she thought childishly, don't let this be happening. I don't want to be here. Let me open my eyes and be back home. Then she opened her eyes, to find herself utterly alone in the bleak Norfolk landscape.

She pressed her hands fiercely to her throbbing temples. Think. She must think—and one stage at a time. The car was out of action, that was obvious even to her inexperienced eyes. Right—she must walk to the village and hope to find a garage. She would arrange for repairs and—then what? She had only intended to stay here an hour or two ... Well, if they couldn't fix the car that afternoon, they could direct her to the pub—there was surely a pub—and she could stay there overnight. Gritting her teeth against the pain in her head and another, more insidious discomfort which was threatening her whole body, she hauled out her handbag and case, took a deep, steadying breath and set off down the quiet lane ...

At the Black Bull, the landlady behaved as though strange, expensively dressed, sun-tanned young women carrying little more than a nightie and toothbrush arrived on her doorstep every day of the week, and Catherine was shown to a pretty, though chill bedroom. She looked at herself in the small mirror, pulled back her hair and was astounded to see a huge, bluish lump on her forehead. She sat on the bed, pulling the heavy eiderdown up round her knees to try to stop the uncontrollable shivering. Perhaps a drink would do her good? An alarming feeling of remoteness was stealing over her. Outside the room, a door banged, a car went past on the road, she heard voices downstairs, but here ... there were only shadows to keep her company.

Catherine swallowed, trying to fight down the feelings of loneliness and isolation, the feeling that absolutely no one knew where she was. The thought of a drink nauseated her, but maybe a couple of painkillers ... clumsily, she tipped out the entire contents of her bag, then slowly picked up—Luke's book. Luke ... Someone she knew ... He despised, hated her, but she would go to him nonetheless. Well, you always intended to, didn't you? No, I didn't, I swear it—it's just that I can't bear being alone ... And she did have one piece of news, at least, that would surely interest him, would even give him a certain ironic amusement . . .

What was it the landlady had said? 'Take the lane past
the church to the end of the village.' She had done that.
The drive for Curlieus—ah, here it was. The rain had
stopped, it was a fine evening, and on the gusting wind
Catherine could hear the sea.

The drive was very long, winding between sombre
rhododendron bushes, and she was grateful when it
widened out to skirt spacious lawns. Curlieus itself was
far bigger than she had imagined, a beautiful old
rambling red-brick house, its walls smothered in ivy and
a spreading yellow rose. She rang the heavy porch bell
and cleared her throat, mentally rehearsing her speech.
Look, Luke, I don't want to intrude, but you see, I feel so
lonely. Couldn't we just forget our differences, spend an
hour laughing over that time I kicked you and you
dumped me in the sea? And then I'll go, I promise. But
the speech was not needed, for no one answered the door.

Luke wasn't at home. Tears sprang to her eyes, but she
closed her lips firmly, refusing to cry. She was already
retreating down the drive when, without warning, a huge
black dog bounded round the corner of the house,
barking ferociously. A woman appeared behind him,
calling, 'Jasper' and the dog, after a final growl, ran back
to her. The woman stood, holding the dog's collar firmly,
as Catherine approached, feeling faintly embarrassed.
She was now wishing desperately that she had not set out
on this crazy venture, but the woman said, pleasantly
enough, 'Can I help you?'

'I was—I was looking for Mr Devinish,' Catherine
stammered.

'Come on in.'

The woman led the way through an arch to a side door.
Inside the hall, what seemed like dozens of dogs of
various shapes and sizes leaped at Catherine, tails

wagging furiously, and even Jasper pushed his cold nose against her hand. The woman made a half-hearted attempt to restrain their exuberance, then gave Catherine a deprecating smile. She was about thirty, pretty in rather a well-bred, vague way, and was dressed in dreadful old jeans and sweater. She opened a door and it seemed to Catherine as though they were both carried through it on a tide of heaving bodies.

She smiled at the woman politely, wishing that her head would stop aching. 'You—like dogs?'

What a trite remark, she thought, but the woman's face lit up and she stooped to fondle Jasper. 'Oh yes—well, they're so much preferable to humans, don't you think?'

There wasn't really an answer to that, so Catherine just smiled again. The room was very cold and when she sat down a cloud of multicoloured dog hairs floated gently up from the sofa.

'I won't be a moment. He's about somewhere—I'll try and find him.'

Catherine leaned back, listening to the footsteps going away down the passage. She was beginning to feel quite awful, she thought, with clinical detachment . . .

'Are you all right?' The woman was looking down at her anxiously, and Catherine forced herself to sit up.

'Oh, yes, thank you.' She felt she had to offer some explanation. 'I—I had a bit of a bump with my car, but I'm fine really.'

'Well, my husband says he's sorry to keep you. He'll be along in a moment.'

'Your—husband!' Catherine had blurted out the words before she could stop herself. So she had been right, after all, Luke was married! Had he been when he was out in St Hilaire? Or had he, perhaps, married since returning home? Either way, it didn't matter. All that mattered was that Luke was married and, before she had had time to adjust her already befuddled mind to come to terms with this fact, she was about to come face to face with him. She lowered her eyes, afraid of the mute misery she would not be able to conceal, then, at the sound of quick footsteps she looked up tremulously, as the door opened.

Her mind was doing strange things. She was going mad. The man was Luke and yet—it wasn't Luke. It was a younger, slighter, *softer* Luke, without the arrogance, the sternness. But he had Luke's quick mind. He took one look at Catherine's face, then laughed.

'I rather think you're looking for the other Mr Devinish—my cousin, Luke. Am I right?'

Catherine nodded dumbly, unable to trust her voice. The two shocks, one after the other, had almost overturned her wits, she thought.

'Oh—I'm sorry,' the woman said. 'Because John was here, I just assumed you wanted him.'

'But—but I don't understand,' Catherine began. A new terror was gripping her. Perhaps Luke had gone— perhaps he was *dead*! 'I—I thought Curlieus was Luke Devinish's home.'

'So it is.' The woman smiled and stooped to pick up a fox terrier that was sniffing round Catherine's ankle. 'It belonged to his parents, but they gave it to him when he got married. John and I just have this end of the house. Luke lives next door, in the main part, with Sally.'

When he got married ... Sally! ... S ... 'To my darling Luke—all my love, S.' The words came unbidden into Catherine's mind, and she stared at the woman, then she groped blindly for her bag and stood up.

'Oh, please wait,' John Devinish said. 'Luke's been up to London—a problem with a case we're handling, but he'll be back soon, I'm sure.'

'Oh, no, no—I can't wait.' Catherine shook her head vehemently, desperate now to get away. Somehow, she must smile at them both, negotiate the acres of carpet, and escape into the night. She handed the woman the book. 'Please give him this—and no, there's no message.'

She got back to the Black Bull and up to her room—she did not quite know how—and sank down slowly on the bed. Her head was pounding and, quite separately, it seemed, the bruise on her forehead was aching, so that she winced as she switched on the bedside lamp. A wash would do her good. She ran cold water into the basin, then washed her hands thoroughly and splashed water over her face, carefully avoiding the bruise.

'To my darling Luke . . . from S.' '. . . Luke lives next door . . . with Sally . . .' What a fool she had made of herself—what a fool she had been to come. It seemed to her that her mind was now working rationally for the first time that day. It was telling her that she couldn't stay, that she must get away, before her heart was broken again. She had plenty of money on her. She would pay for her room and leave. True, she had no car, but someone at the garage would surely drive her to Norwich or King's Lynn, where she could pick up a London train.

Possessed now by a desperate desire for speed, she threw her things into her bag, cramming them in with nervous haste. She had kept on her fur jacket, and now she must put on the little matching hat, tilting it with exaggerated care so that it hid her bruise. From the mirror, a stranger's face peered anxiously out, and she turned away quickly. She must have some air. The carpet *would* keep floating away from her, but at last she reached the window and flung it wide open, drinking in gulps of the cold night air.

When at last she turned back to sit on the bed, she heard raised voices below, then there were footsteps, across the hall and coming upstairs two at a time. Someone's in a hurry, she thought. She picked up the bottle of painkillers, and by dint of great concentration, shook out two tablets on to her palm, just as the bedroom door flew open with a bang. The tablets leaped from her hand and skittered across the carpet. She looked up, frowning with the effort to focus on Luke Devinish, standing in the doorway.

CHAPTER TEN

NEVER taking his eyes off her, Luke came into the room. He banged the door behind him and leaned against it, while Catherine made a movement to get up then decided that maybe it was safer to stay where she was. He stood for a few moments, arms folded, regarding her without speaking. His face was unsmiling—angry, even—and—had there been a flicker of something else? If there was, it had gone. Catherine, all coherent thought swept away, forced herself to meet the intensity of his gaze, her nervous fingers pleating the fine cream wool of her dress.

'H-hello, Luke.'

Her voice sounded oddly remote, as though it were coming from some far-off cellar and he continued to look down at her, that strange expression on his face.

'Well, well—Catherine Hartley. So I was right— somehow, it just had to be you.'

She remembered that at no time had she given her name at the house. 'How did you know?'

A wry smile flickered momentarily across his features—which were surely thinner than she remembered?

'Well, among my undoubtedly wide circle of acquaintances, even I don't know too many young women with hair the colour of heather honey, eyes to match, and a sun tan that goes in one side and out the other. My cousin's description, by the way,' that wry smile again, 'you've quite dazed the poor chap. Pat obviously needs to divert some of her attention from those damned dogs of hers.'

Catherine smiled, focusing on him with some difficulty, while her whole body, apart from her viciously pounding head, seemed to be turning into a peculiar mixture of wood and jelly.

'And just what the hell do you think you're doing here?' His glance roved round the cold, rather cheerless room.

'Well, I had an——'

'Oh, I know all about that.' His voice was rough. He left the door and came to sit down heavily on the bed beside her. 'I've seen your car and spoken to Turner at the garage. You little fool—trying to break your neck yet again! If you'd gone over into that tidal race——' He broke off abruptly. 'Anyway, what I meant was, you're not staying here——'

'No, I'm not. That is, I *was*, but I'd just finished——' What had she just finished doing?

'And how could you have come all this way and not waited to see me?' Surely she must be imagining the raw hurt, quickly smothered, which had been in his voice. 'You had no intention of seeing me, had you? That's why you gave them my book, then sneaked away.'

She certainly was not imagining the anger, but she too felt a spasm of anger at his words. What did he expect her to have done? Saunter next door and say, 'Oh, good evening, Mrs Devinish. I'd like to see your husband when he gets back. I'm in love with him, you see.' Or *was*, she told herself savagely.

The spurt of rage seemed to have done her good, clearing her head and giving her the strength to stand up. She leaned unobtrusively against the bedhead. Get rid of him, the inner voice was saying. Somehow get rid of him—tell him you'll come round to Curlieus in the morning, then as soon as he's gone, get the landlady to phone for a taxi. You must get away . . .

'Anyway, you're not staying here.' He stood up abruptly. 'I'll see Mrs Parsons, then you're coming home with me to Curlieus.'

Coming home to Curlieus. How marvellous that sounded! Just for a moment, Catherine closed her eyes against the weak tears that were threatening. She must

not break down now, or he would feel even more obliged
to take her under his wing. She opened her eyes again.

'No, I'm not, Luke.'

She attempted to infuse firm resolution into her voice
and to meet his gaze coolly, but it was rather difficult
because suddenly there were four Lukes, standing in a
neat row, all watching her with very unfriendly eyes. Will
the real Luke Devinish please step forward? She laughed
nervously, then put her hands to her head as an agonising
sick pain shot through it. She felt her carefully arranged
hat tumble to the floor then heard Luke give a sharp
exclamation. She couldn't bear his anger, not now, when
she would never see him again. It reminded her of
another terrible day which she couldn't quite place. She
put her hands out towards him supplicatingly, then
flinched as Luke—only one again now—seemed to leap
across the room towards her.

'You're ill! Pat said you didn't look well—and Turner
said you'd bumped your head. Why the hell didn't you
tell me?'

He had snatched her up and was holding her to him, so
tightly that she couldn't breathe, couldn't stand, then
very gently he laid her down on the bed and put his hand
on her head for a moment. Then she heard him running
downstairs, shouting imperiously for the landlady.

It was marvellous to be lying down, but she must not
let herself be weak—she had to get away. Still, she would
lie there, just for a little while . . . There were contorted
voices, disembodied in the air around her. Snatches of
conversation floated past like thistledown and she tried
in vain to snatch at them. Then Luke was enfolding her
in something soft and warm.

'I'll send Barnes round tomorrow with your eiderdown . . . Lucky I brought the Range Rover . . .'

Then another voice. 'What a mercy you came to see
her, Mr Devinish . . . I'd no idea . . . If I'd known you
knew her . . .'

Strong arms were cocooning her, lifting her as though

she were weightless. '. . . And if you'll bring down her things to the car . . . Oh, and ring Dr Brooks . . . tell him it's a blow on the head . . . slight concussion and shock, I think . . .'

The car felt warm, almost womb-like . . . Catherine roused herself only once, vaguely aware that she was being carried up a wide flight of stairs. She opened her eyes and looked straight up into Luke's, just a few inches away. There was something important she had to say. 'I—I didn't see the hay meadows.'

'What?' He stopped and looked down at her, his expression strained.

'You know—those hay meadows that you told me about. I didn't see them.'

His face softened momentarily and he smiled down at her, so that, for a second, her headache completely vanished. 'Oh, *those* hay meadows. I'll show you one day—that's a promise, Tiger.'

Then there was another voice, and cool fingers on her forehead, a light shining in her eyes. She turned her head away impatiently, then hands were holding her firmly, a voice she knew was saying, 'Ssh, Cattie, be a good girl.'

The phrases 'agency nurse' and 'cottage hospital' floated past, then that familiar voice—'No!', almost angrily. A slight laugh, then, 'Of course, you may be in for quite a night . . . Sally . . .' There was something about that name but she couldn't quite remember . . . She roused herself finally and opened her eyes to see—*Luke* bending over her. But it couldn't be Luke. She must be hallucinating—Luke had gone home to England . . .

'Ssh,' Luke's voice whispered. 'Go to sleep. I'll be here all night if you need me.'

Several times in the night, she stirred restlessly, and always she seemed to see the same face, near her. Once, he smiled at her and, feeling her eyes fill with tears, she turned her head away.

* * *

Someone was knocking softly at the door. Catherine rolled over drowsily. She opened her eyes and saw a room she had never seen before. She tried to sit up, but then a grey-haired woman was gently pushing her back on to the pillows.

'How are you dear?' Then, as Catherine lay, looking up at her in bewilderment, 'I'm Mrs Barnes, Mr Luke's housekeeper. I've just sent him away to rest for a while. He looks worn out—and I wasn't even here to make up the spare bed, so he's put you here in his room.'

It was all coming back to her. She moved her head gingerly—it was still aching, but that bursting throb and that terrifying light-headed sensation had gone.

'Anyway, dear, are you feeling better?'

Catherine managed a smile. 'Much better, thank you. I must have been an awful nuisance.'

Mrs Barnes drew back the floor-length curtains slightly, then looked down at her critically. 'My, what a nasty bruise you've got!' she exclaimed. 'And you're so pale! But Dr Brooks is coming this afternoon, so he'll see how you are. Now, I've brought you a nice little bit of breakfast, so mind you eat it. It's just orange juice, some toast and honey. You'll like the honey—it's from my husband's bees.'

As she set down the tray, Catherine glanced down and saw, to her amazement, that she was wearing pyjamas—men's navy ones. Mrs Barnes saw her expression and laughed.

'I gather Mr Luke couldn't find your nightie last night——'

Couldn't find her nightie? Did that mean *he* had undressed her? Her case was open on the floor, clothes scattered impatiently around it.

'—so he put you into a pair of his pyjamas.'

Unbidden, the memory returned of her struggling to get Luke into her gaudy beach pyjamas in her bedroom in

Hope's Mill. Well, the tables had been well and truly turned. She felt herself blushing, and hastily reached for her orange juice.

After Mrs Barnes had gone, Catherine looked around at Luke's bedroom. It was just as she would have expected from her knowledge of the man himself, she thought—almost sparsely furnished, the dark blue carpet and curtains, and the cream walls which set off the well polished antique furniture and made the room light and airy, yet also gave it a curiously impersonal, unloved look. The only softening effect was a large and beautiful seemingly original Impressionist oil painting of a woman in a white dress standing alone in a field of scarlet poppies.

The house was silent. Mrs Barnes had opened the window and through it Catherine could hear the same plaintive, haunting cry of sea birds, far out on the marshes, she supposed.

Before the housekeeper returned for the tray, Catherine was fast asleep again and this time she slept through the afternoon, waking only when Mrs Barnes showed in the doctor. He examined her carefully, and was just repacking his bag when Luke arrived. He was dressed in a casual outfit of beige slimfit cords and black fine-knit sweater, and at the sight of him Catherine's heart felt as though it were being tightly squeezed in a vice.

He glanced briefly, almost impersonally down at her, then said, 'Well, how is she?'

The doctor closed his bag and straightened up. 'She's fine—a remarkable recovery. She's got a sore head, but otherwise, pulse, temperature—all fine.' He smiled kindly at Catherine. 'It must be the Norfolk air—it's potent stuff. Or your tender ministrations, Luke.'

'Oh, don't be fooled by her delicate appearance. She's as tough as old boot-leather, aren't you?' They exchanged looks, then their eyes slid past each other.

Dr Brooks turned towards the door. 'Anyway, I've

told Mrs Barnes, she can get up later. Perhaps a warm bath, then have a couple of hours downstairs—but an early night, mind.' He shot a quick glance at Luke. 'And you look as though you can do with one yourself. I gather you had quite a night.'

They went out together and Catherine, straining her ears, heard something about 'two patients', then she caught the name 'Sally'. So that was the reason the house was so quiet—and would also explain why Luke's wife had not been in to see her. Sally was ill too. No wonder Luke looked so pale and strained. All the more reason why *she* should not be here. Well, she would be away soon—the garage owner had promised to do his best to repair her car. Certainly, somehow she would leave in the morning.

In the meantime, she was going to spend the evening with Luke . . . The fact that he hadn't objected to her coming downstairs suggested that his wife was confined to her room. Surely he could not be so insensitive as to bring her and Catherine together. Unless, as was of course very likely, he had not the slightest inkling of her feelings for him. After all, she had tried hard enough to hide them from him . . . But she *was* going to spend this evening alone with Luke—and in years to come she would clasp to her every precious memory of this stolen time . . .

Mrs Barnes helped her bath, clucking over her bruise, which Catherine saw, in the mirror, was now a blend of deep purples and greens. Then she produced her cotton nightie, which had been sent over from the Black Bull, and an old schoolboy-type brown dressing-gown which smelled faintly of mothballs and, incongruously, lavender. As Catherine tied the belt, the housekeeper surveyed her with satisfaction.

'There, that's better than one of his grown-up ones. I always knew his school dressing-gown would come in handy one day. I could never bring myself to throw it away.'

'You've been here a long time, then?'

'Bless you, yes—since Mr Luke was a litle boy. Of course, his parents lived here then.'

'You must have seen some changes.'

'Yes—well, changes come to us all.' Mrs Barnes, who had been chatting happily, shot her a look and closed her mouth firmly on that particular topic. 'Now, would you like Mr Luke to carry you downstairs?'

'Oh, no!' Catherine all but shrank back at her words. 'I'm—I'm fine.' And in fact, apart from a slight headache, she felt perfectly recovered.

Downstairs, Mrs Barnes showed Catherine into the sitting-room, which was lit only by the radiance of a log fire. Luke was standing at a window, looking out at the twilight.

'Here she is, Mr Luke—and mind you don't keep her up too long. Now, I've set the tea tray ready in the kitchen for when you want it. So if there's nothing else, I'll be off. I'll see you in the morning, Miss Hartley—you can have a nice lie in, with it being Sunday.'

'There's no need for you to come in tomorrow, Mrs Barnes,' Luke broke in. 'I'm lunching with my parents, remember? And I can quite easily get Miss Hartley's breakfast.'

'Oh, but I'm——' Catherine began, but Mrs Barnes had gone, leaving her alone with Luke.

For a few moments they stared at each other across the dark room, the flickering flames reflecting in their eyes, then Luke's mouth twisted. He turned away abruptly to switch on a lamp on a low table and to draw the heavy velvet curtains.

'Don't stand by the door all evening.'

He pushed a comfortable-looking armchair nearer to the fire and Catherine sank into it gratefully, for her legs felt suddenly weak. Perhaps, after all, she had not quite recovered from her ordeal of the previous day.

Luke prodded the fire with a brass poker, until a shower of tiny golden sparks leaped up the chimney, then stood leaning his elbow on the carved pine mantelpiece. He looked down at her, his face sombre, his grey eyes withdrawn, and Catherine's heart sank. Where was she to find those wonderful memories that she needed so desperately to take home with her? She had even lost his book which, with a burning intensity, she had clung to for months, and now Luke was simply staring at her, almost as though he didn't see her, as though his thoughts were elsewhere. Perhaps he resented having to entertain her for the evening. She should have stayed in her room—once again, she had created needless heartache for herself. She leaned her head on her hand.

'What's the matter? Does your head hurt still?'

She glanced up at his unsmiling face. 'Oh no—at least, only where the bruise is. I'm fine, really. I shall be able to leave tomorrow.' She felt she must reassure him on that point—he must not be allowed to think that she wanted to trespass on his life a moment longer than was necessary.

To cover her nervous uncertainty, she fingered a copper jug of creamy white chrysanthemums on a table beside her. The crisply pungent perfume rose up to her, making her feel sad, she did not know why—perhaps it was because they were flowers which were always associated with autumn ... She forced herself to speak, though she could not look at him.

'These chrysanthemums are beautiful.'

'Yes—they're Barnes's pride and joy. I've got an old conservatory and he grows them in there.' He gestured with his head towards the window. 'I won't show you tonight—even with the background heating on, it's chilly in there.'

'I'll see it before I go,' she replied, still with her eyes on the flowers.

'Yes—before you go.' There was a slight, almost imperceptible pause, then he went on, 'I'll pick you a bunch of grapes to take with you—they're very good this year. Mrs Barnes should be able to make some wine.'

'Does she make a lot—of wine, I mean?'

'Gallons of the stuff. And it's very good—well, it keeps her husband out of the Black Bull—at least, some evenings.'

'Oh.'

Their eyes met, and for a moment it seemed as though he was trying to flash her an unspoken message.

'Catherine, I——' He hesitated and she felt a shiver of panic. He was going to tell her about his wife, and she was going to have to smile at him, be unconcerned. 'Oh, damn!' He ran his hands through his hair. 'Look, let's have some tea, shall we? Mrs Barnes left a groaning tray in the kitchen, and there'll be trouble if every crumb hasn't disappeared.'

When he had gone, Catherine leaned back in her chair, her eyes half closed against the warmth of the fire. She almost wished that the strange feeling of dulled unreality of the previous day would return, would creep through her like an anaesthetic, slowly numbing her pain. Stop it, stop it, she urged herself silently. Don't think about tomorrow.

She leaped from the chair and leaned, taut as a bow, against the end of the mantelpiece. Beside her were some huge flints, dark and polished as basalt. She took one in her hands, running her fingers across its cold smoothness. If only her heart could be as hard and unyielding, as immune to feeling! To try and calm herself, she made herself look around the room. Until now, she had only been aware of Luke, his presence filling her senses, but now she could see how pleasant the room was—well-proportioned, almost noble, high-ceilinged, with tall windows. Yet, it managed to be a comfortable, homely room, even though every piece of furniture was obviously hand-picked, and very expensive. At the far end was a grand piano, piles of sheet music—mainly jazz, it seemed—scattered over it. She took a piece at random and began stumbling through the tune with one finger.

'Do you play?' Luke was setting down a tray on a low table.

Catherine laughed and pulled a face. 'It sounds like it, doesn't it? No, I never progressed beyond "Chopsticks" and "Baa Baa Black Sheep". But you do?'

He was standing beside her, too close, and she scratched at a note with her nail.

'Well—a bit. Shall I play something for you?'

He sat down on the piano stool and reached for the pile of music. Catherine sat on the arm of a chair just behind him, leaning her head on her hand. It was, just for once, quite safe to watch him, she thought, as he flicked through the titles, frowning slightly in concentration. A lock of dark hair fell forward over his brow and the longing to reach forward and brush it back was almost too much to bear. . . . She lowered her eyes to his hands, those slim, sensitive, still sunburned hands . . . No ring of any description . . . Every married man should wear a ring, she thought, with a bitter spurt of misery.

The firelight was flickering, the soft lights receding, leaving them in a charmed circle of their own, until Catherine felt almost suffocated by the intensity of the emotions the moment was arousing in her. This was madness—*craziness*—she must stop it now! She scrambled to her feet a little shakily.

'No—don't play anything!' Her voice came out much louder than she had intended and he turned to look at her in surprise. 'You'll—you'll disturb your wife!' she stammered. 'I—I mean, she's ill, isn't she?'

She went to move away from him but he put a hand on her wrist, quite gently, though she knew that if she resisted, those fingers would tighten inexorably.

'What do you mean, Catherine?'

His voice was quite expressionless but she felt his grey eyes on her, though she could not meet his gaze.

'Well—your wife—she's ill. I heard you tell the doctor. And—when I came to Curlieus yesterday, your cousin's wife said——'

'What did Pat say?' He had loosed her hand now and was standing over her. '*What* did she say?' he repeated, his voice harsh.

Catherine looked up at him from under her lashes. He was standing between her and the lights, blotting them out, so that he was only a dark, menacing stranger, the easy companion fled.

She licked her lips. 'Well——' she faltered, then stopped. Perhaps his wife was dreadfully ill, something awful. Yes, that was it—he couldn't bear to talk about it.

'Look—I'm sorry if I've upset you, Luke,' she went on timidly, 'but I didn't realise——'

He put his hands on her arms and shook her. 'For God's sake, Catherine—*tell* me. What did Pat say to you?'

She took a deep breath. 'She said——' She frowned. For some reason that she didn't fully understand, it was absolutely vital that she remembered the exact words. 'She said that—that you lived next door—here—with Sally.'

He stared at her for a moment and she braced herself, expecting—she did not quite know what. Savage anger, silence, withdrawal—a curt explanation. What she did not expect though, was that Luke should loose his grip on her, collapse on to the piano stool, put his head back—and laugh.

Catherine stood watching him in utter amazement. Then, as the laughter went on, she said stiffly, 'Excuse me—I seem to have said something amusing. I'm sorry.'

She went to move away but he seized her hand and got to his feet, still laughing.

'It's not funny—not at all funny,' she said coldly, and

he made an effort to control his mirth.

'No—it's just that—oh, God, Catherine Hartley, was there ever such a little idiot as you?'

He shook her hand, but she snatched it away. With as much dignity as she could muster, she walked over to the tea tray, but as she knelt down at the table he pulled her to her feet again.

'Come on,' he said, his voice still unsteady.

'But the tea's stewed——'

'Damn the tea—come on!'

He pulled her out of the room and along a passage, then threw open a door, gesturing her through and flicking down a switch. They were in the kitchen—a lovely, welcoming room, all glowing pine units and green and blue Greek rugs. He shut the door and leaned against it, his arms folded, as she looked at him uncertainly.

'It's—it's beautiful, but why——?'

'Why have I brought you here? Well, you wanted to meet Sally, didn't you?'

She didn't understand. He was playing games with her, yet again, and she was quite out of her depth. There was a faint snuffle from the far end of the kitchen and Catherine, startled, looked round. The big Aga cooker was sending out a gentle glow of warmth, and beside it was—a dog, a golden labrador, curled up in a wicker basket. Catherine did not see the puppies until she knelt down, then she looked up at Luke, wide-eyed.

'Oh—they're lovely.'

He knelt beside her and the dog nuzzled against his hand lovingly. 'Catherine—meet Sally.'

Utterly speechless, she gaped at him and Luke leaned over and gently closed her lips. At last she found her voice and said slowly, 'But—why did your cousin's wife make me think that——?'

She broke off and there was a faint tinge of resentment in her voice. Luke laughed, this time without amusement.

'Well, I wasn't there, of course, and I don't exactly know what she said to you, but surely, even on a short acquaintance, it's obvious that Pat is—how shall I put it?—more interested in dogs than humans. I'm only surprised if she mentioned me first—she certainly thinks more of Sally!' He smiled wryly at her, but then his expression changed. 'But anyway, what made you jump to that particular conclusion?'

'Well——' She stopped, but it was no use. She must force herself to go on. 'It was your book, that book of John Donne. You know—"To Luke from—from S." I just assumed,' she said lamely and managed an apologetic smile.

'Of course—the book.' Did she imagine it, or was there a frisson of something in his voice? He went on, 'As for what you heard—or half heard—of my conversation with Dr Brooks, well, Sally started in labour last night and as it was her first litter, I wanted to be around. But you did very well, didn't you?' he said, softly scratching the dog's head. She gave him an adoring look in return, then went on licking one of the puppies all over. 'Quite a night—I think that's what I said. And that was an understatement—you all pale and ghostly upstairs and the labour ward down here. Yes, quite a night.'

Catherine put a tentative hand down and absently stroked the dog's soft fur. Her mind was refusing to function properly—but she clung on to one overwhelming thought—Luke wasn't married, after all. Luke wasn't married . . . It was like a joyous refrain, first in her brain, then like a piece of cut glass which has been lightly struck, echoing all through her body.

She became aware that Luke had gently lifted out one of the pups. He put it in her cupped hands, and as she held the tiny, sleeping creature she smiled up at him, bright-eyed.

'Oh, I've never seen such a young puppy. It's beautiful. But it's black and——'

'Yes, that bloody Jasper is the father! I knew it—whatever Pat, hand on heart, might swear to the contrary, that evil ruffian lay in wait—well, we won't bother with any of the sordid details!'

As Catherine gently replaced Jasper junior, she stroked her finger along the tiny black muzzle.

'Would you like him, Catherine?' Luke's voice was matter of fact. 'You can have him if you like.'

Her face lit up for a moment, then clouded. 'Oh, Luke, I'd have loved him—I've never had a dog. Thank you. But—it's impossible. I—I shall have to go back to London tomorrow—I'm—I'm flying back to St Hilaire on Monday.'

He shrugged carelessly. 'Oh, well, it was just an idea. Monday! I wondered if you were over here to stay.'

'Oh, no—I just came over for a few days. But thank you, anyway.'

'That's OK.' His voice was cool, off-hand even. She had obviously offended him by her refusal, but what else could she have done?

'Anyway, let's leave them to it. Look, I'll fetch out that tray—the tea'll be ruined but I'll make us some more. You go and sit by the fire.' . . .

Catherine licked the butter from her fingers. 'Mmm, lovely. What a pity they don't have muffins at home. But I suppose they're very fattening—most nice things are.'

He passed her the plate. 'I shouldn't worry about that—you've lost weight.'

'So have you.' The words were out before she could stop them. 'I—I mean, you *look* as though you have.' Their glances locked again, then she tore her eyes from his and picked up her tea cup. 'I'm sorry, Luke,' she began, 'I mean about—getting everything so mixed up. It was stupid of me and—well, I might have hurt you. If you *had* had a wife, that is——'

She glanced across at him and saw, in the firelight,

momentarily, the harsh lines etched once more round his eyes and mouth.

'I've said the wrong thing again,' she said flatly.

'No—not at all. How could you know?' He spoke sombrely, the laughter all gone now. 'Oh, yes. I *was* married—for ten years. My wife——'

'Don't go on, Luke!' she burst out, as though afraid of what she would hear. 'It's nothing to do with me—or anyone else.'

But he ignored her interrruption. 'Yes, I want to tell you, Catherine—you above everyone.'

They had been sitting side by side on the sofa whilst they ate their tea, wrapped in a companionable warmth, but now Luke slipped down, to lean against it, staring at the fire, his face bleak, his eyes remote. He was still near her, yet Catherine would not for worlds have touched him, for he had gone a very long way away.

'I met Sara at Oxford.' He flicked her a glance. 'Yes, that's right—S, for Sara. We were both in the University Drama Society.' He smiled ironically. 'Of course, you've seen a little of my talent in that direction! Well, I fell for her hard. She was very beautiful, with a sort of brilliant personality—the kind of girl who would make all others seem somehow insignificant by contrast. I suppose you realise that I'm—fairly wealthy?' She nodded. 'Mainly through the efforts of my father, who was a real high-flier in his day—made his first million by thirty, when there weren't all that many thirty-year-old millionaires about. Sara saw herself married to a rich, international socialite, with a glittering life-style, one of the beautiful people.

'When I told her I had no intention at all of living my life like that, that I was not just studying law for kicks but I actually intended to practise it, she chose not to believe me—or thought she would very easily persuade me otherwise after we were married.' His voice was bitter. 'She just couldn't understand. I'd been dispatched to boarding-school at the earliest opportunity, and my mother led a lonely life—true, it was filled with all the trappings of success that it's possible to fill one single life with—this house, a flat in London, a luxury cruise every winter—but still lonely. She would never admit it, of course, but I'm sure she privately considers my father's near-fatal heart attack the best thing that's ever happened to her. It forced him to retire at the age of fifty.'

He shot her a quirky smile, then it faded abruptly, leaving his face shuttered once more. 'Anyway, I had no intention of going the same way, and my father understood—at least, he did in the end.' His voice was dry. 'He told me that if that was what I wanted, just to make sure I was the best bloody lawyer around. He and I still have a controlling interest in two of the family firms.

'But Sara didn't see things that way. She had a comfortable enough life—my parents handed over Curlieus, and the London flat, when we married, and she could have everything she asked for—except the one thing she really craved for—a life-style with the international jet-set, going off all over the world, being seen in all the right places at all the right times, dinner parties for glossy people, with her playing the glamorous hostess. But I'd seen too much of it when I was young, you see, to want it for myself.'

There was a hurt in his voice which made Catherine lift her hand and, hardly knowing what she was doing, rest it on his shoulder.

'Don't tell me any more,' she said quietly. 'It's nothing to do with me—and it's too painful for you.'

'But I want to tell you—I owe it to you,' he said, almost angrily. 'Well, to cut it short—she was restless, moody, she said I was stifling her—and maybe I was—so she took up acting again. With a bit of talent, and her looks, she managed to pick up the odd part here and there— mainly through my influence, although she never knew that, of course. She even had a bit part in two or three episodes of a TV soap, I seem to remember.'

His voice was off-hand. He might have been reciting another couple's story for all the emotion he showed. 'Anyway, the crunch came when I wanted very much to start a family. Sara refused. We quarrelled, she went off to one of the French film festivals and was picked up by a playboy who calls himself a film director. She only called back here to collect all her belongings,' he said drily, 'and to have one final venomous go at me, then she followed him to Miami, where she was going to divorce me, marry him, and be turned overnight into *the* star of the decade. At least, that was her intention—I don't think it's quite worked out that way, so far.'

'Who was this director?' Catherine whispered. 'Is he well known?'

'Well,' Luke gave her a twisted smile. 'His name just may be familiar to you. It's Brannan—Vince Brannan.'

CHAPTER ELEVEN

CATHERINE gasped. 'You mean—*the* Brannan—of Brannan International?'

'The same,' Luke nodded. 'Well—at least, his son. I think Sara saw him as her passport into the really big time—fame *and* fortune, unlimited.'

Catherine looked at him, her heart constricting with pity. His tone was laconic, even flippant, but, alive as she was to his every nuance, she sensed the pain. How in the world had a *proud* man like Luke Devinish been able to withstand such a blow?

'I arranged a meeting with her in Miami, where she told me the divorce papers were already filed—on the grounds of my neglect, I gather.' That dry, unemotional tone again. 'I cabled home to say they must manage without me for a while, bought an old sailing boat and got as far as Barbados, where I met up with Steve Bennet. He told me about their attempts to buy a little beach in St Hilaire, in the teeth of powerful opposition from the Brannans. That added, shall we say, a certain piquancy, and anything I could do in the line of anti-Brannan sabotage——' He shrugged. 'Between us, we cooked up the squatter scheme and, well, you know the rest.'

They were both silent, as in the grate a log burst in a shower of sparks and subsided into ash. Although she had tried to stop him, Catherine was glad that he had told her. She understood now why he had behaved in the way he had—everything now fitted into place. Tomorrow, she thought, she would be leaving Curlieus, and Luke. Yet strangely, she felt no pain or sadness. It was as though tonight—was enough. Luke beside her, the mellow, comfortable warmth, the firelight, the scent of the chrysanthemums, even the rain which was now beating against the windows—everything had come together suddenly into one perfect, magic, totally satisfying moment.

'Catherine.'

She turned to look at him, struck by the deep seriousness in his voice. He leaned forward and took both her hands in his.

'Catherine, I want to tell you something.' Her eyes were locked with his, and she could not turn away. 'Just because I've been unlucky once—in marriage, I mean—it doesn't mean that I——'

She jumped as the telephone shrilled and Luke, cursing softly, got up to answer it. 'Linda, hello. How are you?' His voice was constrained, and he glanced across at Catherine. 'Look, hang on a minute, Linda.' He put his hand over the receiver and turned to Catherine. 'Sorry—it's business. I'll take it on the extension, then it won't disturb you.'

He went out, but reappeared a few moments later, carrying a bottle and a glass which he set down beside her.

'Nearly forgot. Strict instructions from Mrs Barnes—you're to have a glass of her home-made blackcurrant wine. She thinks you look anaemic or something. But not much, mind—it's heady stuff. I'll be as quick as I can, but this call from Linda—it's a bit complicated because she's an old friend of mine. Poor kid—her husband's cleared off, and she's in a bit of a state over the divorce settlement, which I'm handling for her.'

The door banged behind him but clicked open again and Catherine heard him say, 'Now, Linda, for heaven's sake calm down, and tell me what he's been doing now.' She tiptoed to the door and closed it softly, feeling an intense reluctance to eavesdrop further.

She poured herself a glass of wine, switched off the table lamp, put on another log then hunched on the rug, clasping her knees and looking into the flames. 'Linda, . . . an old friend of mine . . .' Luke and Linda— yes, they went together somehow, sounded right. Was this what he had been about to tell her? Perhaps, after all, in spite of all her care, he had guessed something of her feelings for him, and had been going to tell her, as gently as he could . . .

Catherine shivered. The warmth, the magic, was melting away into the shadows at the far end of the room, and she knew with sudden clarity why. It had been nothing to do with tea beside a cosy log fire on a wet September evening—it had been magic only because Luke was there, and now he had gone. She stared into the red heart of the fire with dry, tearless eyes, as a bleak, desolate unhappiness seeped through her whole body.

She took a long sip at her wine. Mmm, lovely. She held up the glass to the fire and the wine glowed softly, like purple velvet. How fitting, she thought. Purple, the colour of mourning—mourning for her love. 'You're getting maudlin, my girl,' she said aloud, and reaching for the bottle, poured herself another generous drink. It trickled down her throat like warm, soothing fire. Strong stuff? Rubbish—how could blackcurrants be strong? Besides, she was beginning to feel better, better than she had done for months. She must have been—what was it?— anaemic, after all. She topped up her drink, took a gulp, then raised her glass in salute. Good old Mrs Barnes . . .

Luke was standing over her, and she blinked up at him.

'Sorry I was so long. Damned nerve really, ringing me up at home on business, but she was rather overwrought. Has been ever since this thing blew up, and she seems to think that, with my first-hand experience, I'm an expert at sorting out messy divorces.' The bitterness in his tone momentarily broke through the pleasant haze in Catherine's mind. 'Anyway,' he went on, 'I've told her to come into the office next week, so let's forget her.'

Damned nerve ... let's forget her! Well, Catherine thought, I needn't have worried on that score. He doesn't exactly seem to be talking about the next Mrs Devinish!

Luke squatted down beside her on his haunches as Catherine carefuly set down her glass and leaned her head against the arm of the sofa. In the firelight, he was even more handsome, the hard planes of his face softened, the lines of tension which were always round his mouth and eyes smoothed away, as they had been that night at Hope's Mill. But that night, she had only wanted to hold him, take care of him. Now? What did she want now? She felt her breathing becoming more and more shallow and unsteady. She smiled up at Luke then, as he looked back at her unsmilingly, put up her hand and brushed her fingers, butterfly-gently, across his warm lips.

The next moment, Luke took a sharp breath, then pulled her roughly towards him and buried his face in her hair. After a few moments, he lifted his head and stared down into her eyes. Catherine, her whole body alive to his nearness, loosed all reserve. She smiled up at him lazily and his eyes darkened in response. He lowered his head and kissed her with a kind of scarcely subdued violence. She felt his mouth moving against hers, his tongue thrusting between her lips, and she closed her eyes. Sliding her hands under his sweater, she pressed him closer to her. At last he raised his head to look at her and Catherine, clasped in his arms, felt a delicious voluptuousness pervading her whole body. She gave him a languid smile, from under her lashes.

'Oh, God, Catherine.' He gave a shaky laugh. 'Don't look like that, or I won't be responsible for my actions.'

She went on smiling at him, then, without warning, gave a loud hiccup. She clasped her hand to her mouth and looked at him, wide-eyed.

'Sorry about——' she began, then hiccuped again, even louder.

He drew back from her and caught hold of her shoulders, subjecting her to a narrow-eyed scrutiny until she felt quite uncomfortable.

'How much have you had to drink?' he demanded.

'Oh, not very much really,' she mumbled. For some reason, it seemed difficult to speak clearly and she had to enunciate each word with great care.

'Hmm.' He looked at her, then leaned over and picked up the bottle. He tilted it to the fire, then stared at her.

'You've guzzled nearly half the bottle,' he said accusingly.

'Why not?' she replied belligerently. He was being so unreasonable—as usual. After all, she was anaemic, wasn't she? She *needed* it. 'Anyway, it's only like baby's fruit juice,' she added sulkily.

'Give me strength,' he rolled his eyes ceilingwards, 'Mrs Barnes's ten-year-old wine, and she says it's baby's fruit juice! That wine—it's at least as potent as any of your island brews. Why do you think Barnes has got hairs on his chest like coconut matting?'

How handsome he was when he frowned. Catherine put up her hand and caressed his cheek.

'Please, Luke,' she said softly, but he leaped to his feet and regarded her sternly, hands on hips.

'Get up.'

'Why?'

'Because if you continue to look at me like that, you'll undermine my New Year resolution never to make love to a girl who's too drunk to know what she's doing.'

'I'm—not drunk,' she said crossly. He was spoiling everything.

'Well—tipsy then. And don't pout. Come on.'

He placed his hands under her arms and lifted her

effortlessly to her feet. She put a hand on the
mantelpiece, to steady herself ever so slightly, and
regarded him coldly.

'You know s-something, Luke Devinish,' she remarked. 'I h-hate you. I always have done, and I always
will.'

His lips twitched momentarily, but he just said, 'I'll
help you upstairs.'

He put his hand on her arm, but she shook it off,
saying, 'I can manage perfectly, thank you.'

At the foot of the stairs he said, 'What are you going to
do?'

'I'm going to have a bath and go to bed.'

'You're not to have a bath in your state.'

'Oh, mind your own—all right, *all right*,' she said
hastily. Being the perfect gentleman that he was, she
knew he was quite capable of dragging her bodily out of
the bath if she disobeyed him. 'I'll just have a shower—
will that satisfy you?'

'I should make it a cold one.'

He leaned against the banister, watching her careful
progress, and when she reached the landing, he called,
'Oh, by the way——'

She looked down the long staircase to where he stood,
darkly outlined against the light.

'Yes?'

'I forgot to tell you—Mrs Barnes has prepared the
guest-bedroom for you. It's along the landing, past my
room. She didn't seem to think it was quite proper for you
to be in my bed, even if I wasn't occupying it at the time.
Goodnight, Tiger—sleep well.'

And he was gone, closing the sitting-room door behind
him as though to cut off any further contact with her.

The guest-room, lit by rose-pink shaded wall lights, was
charming, almost like a stage set. Catherine closed the

door and leaned against it, looking round. The room was at the far end of the house, with windows on two sides, and although the heavy green velvet curtains were tightly closed tonight, in summer it would be light and airy. The thick sea-green carpet was almost spongy under her feet, the walls were a delicate floral of blue and green, setting off the pale wood furniture. Beside the bed was an electric blanket lead, the switch glowing orange, and when she put her hand on the pink bedspread a friendly warmth met her touch. Marvellous . . . to curl up in a snug, comforting bed. And, for some reason, she was in need of a little comfort, she thought wryly.

Her head was still spinning slightly, but the effects of the wine could not blot out entirely the angry shame she was feeling. How could she have done it? More or less offered herself to him—and only so that he could reject her, humiliate her, as he had done so often in the past. Was it misplaced jealousy over the phone call with Linda—or had she done it only out of pity for his past unhappiness? She wanted to convince herself that this was the reason, but she knew it was not so. Well—only a few more hours, and he would never be able to reject her again—never.

The bed beckoned, the orange switch-light a beacon. Perhaps she would lie down, just for a few minutes, then shower later . . .

'Catherine, what are you doing?'

She half opened her eyes and squinted up at Luke.

'I'm asleep,' she said briefly, and closed her eyes again.

'With the lights blazing, and the blanket switched on?' He laughed softly. 'In Norfolk we tend to sleep under the covers, not on top of them.' His voice was dry.

He scooped her up into his arms and she laid her head against his chest. He pulled back the bedclothes and dumped her on to the red-hot mattress, then pulled up the bed clothes round her, as she buried her nose in the pillow.

'Lucky I looked in to check that you were all right. You'd have been sizzled by morning. Sleep tight.'

He rested his hand on her head for an instant, then the room was plunged into darkness and a few seconds later, just as she plunged down into a vortex of sleep, she heard the door softly close.

CHAPTER TWELVE

CATHERINE reached across and felt for the bedside light switch, then looked at her watch. A few minutes to five ... *five a.m.*! What a time to wake. She rolled on to her back and stretched luxuriously. Vintage blackcurrant wine, Norfolk air, just sheer fatigue; whatever the reasons, she had slept like a log and, just for a moment, she felt—wonderful. But then, the memories of the previous evening—her own abandoned behaviour, and Luke's determined dismissal of her, seeped back into her mind. How could she have been so unutterably stupid?

She flung herself over on the bed. What should she do? Just lie there until Mrs Barnes brought her a cup of tea in about three hours' time? No—impossible. She would have a leisurely bath, wash her hair perhaps—the previous night, her brain had just about registered a wall hairdrier in the bathroom that led off her room. Then, maybe, she would draw the curtains and silently watch for the dawn. She pinned up her hair, then peeled off her nightie and went through to the bathroom.

After her bath, and wrapped in a pink bath sheet, she padded back into the bedroom to find the shampoo in her overnight bag. She sat down at the dressing-table and slowly began pulling out the pins in her hair, absently shaking it down round her shoulders. This time tomorrow, if Mr Turner kept his word and the car was ready, she would be back in London—maybe packing, as she would be doing here in just a little while. Was she glad? Was she sorry? She didn't know—it was as though she were suspended by a thread in mid-air, above all emotion—but waiting ...

There was a peremptory knock at the door and Luke

came in. The dressing-table was out of line with the door
and he did not at first see her. Then his head jerked round
as Catherine, clutching the bath towel, stared at him in
the mirror. His dark hair was dishevelled from sleep, and
he was still belting the tie of his navy velour robe.

'I thought I heard you moving about. You're not ill
again, are you?'

'Oh, no. I'm sorry if I disturbed you.' She spoke to a
spot just beside his right ear, for she knew she could not
meet his eye. 'I feel fine, but I woke early, so I decided to
have a bath.'

She picked up her comb and ran her nail along its edge,
slowly, so that each separate tooth sprang back. Why
didn't he go? His presence was filling the room,
disturbing her, but when her eyes slid momentarily to her
own reflection she was relieved to see that she looked
perfectly composed. He could not possibly guess at the
whirlwind of emotions that the mere sight of him had set
spinning inside her once again.

'And no hangover?'

'No—not in the least.' Somehow she managed to meet
his steady gaze. 'I wasn't at all drunk, you know. I just
felt—a bit dizzy.'

Too late, she realised that it would have been
preferable for him to think that she had been more tipsy
than she really was—it would, after all, have been the
perfect excuse for her behaviour downstairs, which she
now so bitterly regretted.

Holding firmly on to the towel, she stood up and faced
him across the carpet. 'At least, well—perhaps I was a bit
tipsy—I'm not used to home-made wine.'

She put on a shamefaced smile and Luke's grey eyes
regarded her levelly, a penetrating look, so that she felt
the colour rise in her cheeks. She scuffed her toe
nervously in the carpet, wishing only that he would go—
leave her alone. Having played—and won—that long,
painful game with her in St Hilaire, surely, surely, he

wasn't still playing with her here?

She tried to look coolly back at him. He needed a shave, just as he had done that morning on Mangrove Cay. No—don't think of that! But she found herself aching to caress him; if only she could put out her hand as she had done the previous night and gently——Horrified, she caught herself up. Last night, there had been the excuse of the alcohol; this morning there was no excuse whatever. Besides, it would only invite his derision once more—she must show him that she too was quite immune.

'You should always wear it like that, you know.'

'What?' She stared at him blankly.

'Your hair. You should always wear it down—it suits you much better.' His tone was very light, but his eyes were sombre.

'Oh, don't you like it up?' She fought to make her voice casual, lifted her free hand and, catching up her tumbled hair, swept it clear of her neck. 'It's so much more sophisticated this way—it's how all the most successful Port Charlotte businesswomen are looking this autumn.'

She looked at him under her arm for a moment, then, as she saw his expression, her brittle smile faded and her hair dropped back, unnoticed, round her shoulders.

'Oh, God, Catherine, I've told you—don't—look—at—me—like—that! You must know I can hardly keep my hands off you. Last night, I wanted you so badly it was as much as I could do not to——' He broke off, compressing his lips as though in anger.

Then, as Catherine continued to stare at him, her breasts rising quick and shallow under her rapid breathing, he gave an incoherent exclamation and, catching her by her shoulders, pulled her roughly into his arms. For an instant, his head was between her and the light, then his lips, hard and demanding, were on hers, one hand behind her head, the other against her back, straining her closer to him, as though to fuse their two bodies in molten heat. His tongue was in her mouth, and she closed her eyes against the sweetness, melting under him.

He held her away from him and, catching hold of the bath towel, pulled her free of it so that, looking down, she saw her body, glowing gold in the soft light. Their eyes met, his dark and intent, then he put his hands lightly on her waist and, very deliberately, lowered his head, his lips brushing in a long trail of soft fire from her lips, down the side of her throat and over the rounded curve of her breast, until they reached one quivering centre. Then he raised his head again and looked at her.

'Cathy?'

His voice shook and Catherine could only smile gently back at him, her lips trembling. Question, answer— given and received. The old, unspoken message flashed between them—no need for more words. She was being snatched up, laid down gently on the bed, and Luke was beside her, against her, their damp skin blazing with heat. At every new touch, brilliant fireworks exploded deep inside her, as a wild, drowning joy filled her whole mind and body with a sense of absolute rightness. That first moment on Coral Strand, when he had looked up at her, that intangible something flashing between them . . . and now, the consummation of that moment. Never mind tomorrow, I love you, love you, love you . . . The words were echoing in her brain and she clung to him, surrendering her body to him, with only the faintest sigh as he entered her.

Then his surging passion, caught up on a flood tide that left her far behind, a long, shuddering gasp, and he lay still on her, his dark head on her breast, her arms around him.

At last he raised his head and looked at her, a long, wordless look. The lines of strain had eased from his mouth and when she smiled up at him, tremulously, he bent his head and kissed her, a velvet, gentle kiss.

'Thank you,' he said softly, against her mouth.

'For what?' she whispered.

'You know. But I'm sorry. If I'd known, I'd have been more—more gentle, have waited for you——'

'Would you?' Her eyes glinted in a teasing smile, and he pulled a wry face.

'Well—perhaps not. But as it is——'

He took her hand and began softly kissing the palm, brushing his lips across her moist skin, along each finger to its pink tip, until her flesh quivered under the erotic assault, first of his lips, then of his tongue. He moved from her hand across to her breast and she gave a tiny shiver. Delicious, yet almost frightening sensations began gently, almost imperceptibly to stir very deep within her, as he caressed her skin, his hands and lips moving over her body, down towards the centre of her being, arousing more and more sensation, until she shuddered with desire. It was as though she had lost all volition of herself, as he drew from her deeper and deeper responses and feelings that she had not known herself capable of, until it almost seemed to her that she was vibrating softly under his fingers. *No*—he was killing her, she couldn't bear it. Oh, yes, *yes*, Luke, I want you . . .

This time, she too was caught up in the roaring tide, caught up, and hurtled along as Luke's body, the feel of him, the smell of him, seemed to pervade all her senses. She clenched her fingers on his shoulders and heard someone—herself?—call his name, as the flood broke inside her and dashed her down on some distant shore. Then, shaken, their passion spent, they clung wordlessly to each other.

Catherine, opening her eyes just once, looked round the room and thought, nothing surely will ever matter again. Beyond this moment, this room, nothing will ever quite . . .

* * *

She was being jolted out of some marvellous, evanescent
dream. She yawned drowsily, half opening her eyes
against the brightness which was filtering into the room,
even through the drawn curtains. Then, as she remembered, her eyes flew wide open and she turned her head
sharply, expecting to see Luke.

But beside her there was only an empty, rumpled space
and a faint indentation still in the pillow, to show where
he had lain. Of Luke himself there was no sign—even his
clothes had gone, she realised. It was almost—almost as
though it had been a dream. Luke. At the thought of him,
her heart contracted. She had thought she loved him
before, but now ... And surely, *surely* he must feel
something for her after that shared closeness, when they
had taken each other's bodies, almost becoming each
other in the intensity of their entwined emotions.

Catherine lay very still. She wanted Luke most
desperately to come—she willed him to come, to take her
in his arms again, to reassure her. She buried her face for
a moment against his pillow, where the faintest hint of
his aftershave still lingered tantalisingly, as it also
lingered on her warm skin, sensual as a perfume.

Then, over the rounded pillow, she caught sight of the
small bedside clock. Almost eleven o'clock. *Eleven*! She
sat bolt upright. Why hadn't Luke woken her, or at least
waited for her to waken, instead of going off silently,
even furtively? It was almost as though—she tried to
thrust the unpleasant thought from her—as though he
had wanted to escape from her. But wait a minute. Yes—
Mrs Barnes. He had woken first and, considerate of her
feelings, had slipped away so that she should not be
embarrassed when the housekeeper brought her
breakfast.

She got slowly out of bed and slipped on her nightie.
The pink bath sheet was still lying on the carpet where
Luke had let it fall. She laid it on a chair, then drew back
the curtains from the huge side window and flung it open.

Mmm, a marvellous morning—warm, mellow sunshine and a clear blue sky after the rain. Her senses were sharpened, so that the air felt clean, almost scented, like wine, and she leaned against the window-frame taking in deep gulps of it and hugging herself in a kind of ecstasy. In the distance she could hear church bells and nearer, as ever, the discordant cry of gulls. Church bells ... Sunday ... 'There's no need for you to come in tomorrow, Mrs Barnes.'

Without warning, Luke's words of the previous evening came back to her and for a moment she stood very still. Then——Of course, that was it. At this very moment he was downstairs preparing her breakfast tray. Well, she would surprise him.

She showered quickly, then, impatient to be with him, she pulled on the only other outfit she had brought with her—white canvas jeans and a loose, bright pink mohair sweater, and went down, almost skimming each stair. She went into the kitchen, but the room was empty, apart from Sally and the puppies, still fast asleep and snuffling quietly in the gentle warmth from the cooker. A percolator and a tin of coffee beans stood on the pine table, but everything else was just as it had been the previous night.

Catherine stood for a moment, biting her lip and drumming a rhythm with her fingers on the lid of the coffee tin. Then she went down the passage and opened the sitting-room door. But the heavy velvet curtains were undrawn, the room still in darkness, so she switched on the light. Nothing had been touched. The blazing log fire, which had so comforted and warmed her, was now a ruin of grey ash, while the bottle of blackcurrant wine and her glass still stood on the stone hearth.

She switched off the light, closed the door carefully, and stood in the passage, listening. An old clock ticked steadily, a floorboard creaked, but otherwise the house was silent, so that when one of the late roses in a vase on the oak dresser beside her fell, scattering its brownish petals across the polished wood, she jumped.

Luke was not in the house, and some instinct told her that she would not find him outside in the grounds either. She leaned against the wall, her fingers idly picking at the leathery rose petals, as her eyes blurred with tears. Luke was not there, and she knew why. He regretted their lovemaking and now, still scarred and unable to face any further emotional entanglement, perhaps horrified, even guilty, at what had happened, he had chosen this way to show her. True, he was physically attracted to her, but that was all, and now that that attraction had perhaps been assuaged a little, he wanted to end their relationship.

And it was not his fault, she told herself fiercely, not in the least. After all, he had never pretended to love her. Even this morning, he had not said, 'Catherine, I love you', the words he had, in her imagination, whispered to her so many times since he had coldly turned his back on her at the airport, rejecting her, as he was rejecting her now. So, thinking that this way was, in the end, less cruel, he had gone, to let her realise the truth alone.

In the silent hall she said aloud, 'What shall I do?'

Beside her, the telephone rang and Catherine, almost like an automaton, picked up the receiver.

'I'm sorry,' she said, 'Mr D-Devinish isn't here.' She barely recognised her own voice.

'Is that Miss Hartley?'

'Y-yes.'

''Morning, Miss. Turner's Garage here. I was just ringing to say your car's ready. So you'll be able to get back to London today. Will you be wanting it this morning?'

Of course. Her question had been answered. Luke wanted it and, loving him, she must do as he wished. She cleared her throat of an obstruction which threatened to choke her.

'Yes, I shall, thank you.' Her voice was quite steady now. 'I'll be along in—how long does it take to walk from Curlieus to the village?'

'Oh, about twenty minutes.'

There was a faint surprise in his voice, but Catherine only said quickly, 'I'll be there in half an hour.'

She replaced the receiver very precisely. Then, as though to shatter the silent emptiness of the house and, at the same time, relieve the almost unbearable need to cry, she spun round and raced up the stairs, her footsteps echoing. Back in her room, she threw her things into her overnight bag, pulled at the zip in such clumsy haste that it jammed, then dragged on her jacket and hat, and ran back downstairs.

As she closed the front door behind her, a dog barked at the far end of the house and her heart beat faster with apprehension. She simply couldn't face Pat or John . . . their questions . . . trying to persuade her to wait . . . But no one appeared.

Down the drive, out at last into the lane to the village. There were the hay meadows . . . 'Cowslips and lady's smocks in spring . . . show you some day, Tiger . . .' Don't linger, must get on—get to the garage. This dreadful, aching pain that was threatening to take over her whole body, it would ease once she was in the car and driving away, she was sure of that. She hunched up her shoulder bag, then set off at a steady pace. On each side of her the hedges glowed with hawthorn berries, while wasps, lurching among overripe blackberries, droned drunkenly. It was warm in the lane, too warm in her jacket. She hoped she would reach the village soon.

She heard a car coming fast down the lane behind her so she squeezed up against the hedge to let it pass, a bramble dragging across her leg. Then, as the car shot past her and screamed to a halt, she gave a convulsive start and half turned as though to run. But Luke was out of the car and to her. He stood in front of her, his hands on his hips, scowling furiously at her, so that Catherine, terrified by the anger in his face, tightened her grip on her bag as though for protection. He snatched it from her and hurled it into the road.

'And just where the bloody hell do you think you're going?'

'To the garage, of course.' She jutted her chin out, in an attempt to match his hectoring manner.

To her astonishment, he put his head back and laughed. She regarded him balefully. 'I don't see what's so funny about that.'

She snatched up her bag and began almost running down the lane, in her frantic haste to escape from him. Where *was* the village? Surely she should be there by now—or at least be in sight of the church tower? The church—sanctuary—yes, that was it, she thought crazily, if she could reach the church, she could lock herself in and claim sanctuary! But Luke, with his long legs, caught her up in a few yards and, putting his arm round her waist, whirled her round to him.

'What's so funny,' he exclaimed, 'is that you're going the wrong way—you're trekking as hard as you can out towards the salt marshes and the sea. The village is right behind you!'

Catherine looked round and saw, with a sinking heart, the church tower in the distance. There was nowhere to run to. She was trapped—and by her own stupidity. Luke relinquished his hold on her and held out his hand.

'Give me that bag.'

'No.' She watched, tight-lipped, as he carefully prised her fingers from around the handles then, dragging her behind him, he threw it on to the back seat of the car.

'Now—get in.'

'No, I will not, and give me my——'

'Get in, or I'll throw you in on top of it.'

She looked up at him defiantly then, seeing the glint in his eyes, hastily scrambled in. She sat staring straight

ahead as Luke slammed the door, then slid in beside her
and started the powerful engine. But instead of reversing
up the lane, the car shot forward.

'Look—you can turn in that gateway,' she said, but
Luke only lifted one eyebrow and went on driving—not
recklessly, but fast enough down the narrow ribbon of
lane.

After half a mile or so the road petered out beside a
winding creek and he pulled up, the wheels almost on the
shimmering mud. He leaned forward and switched off
the engine, and for a moment the only sound was the
wind, rustling gently among the tall reeds which
stretched to the horizon.

'Why have you brought me here?' Her voice was
strained. Why was he prolonging it? And why hadn't he,
after all, been content just to let her go? Didn't he realise
that it would be far, far harder for her now that she had
seen him again? Perhaps he was merely playing one last,
cruel game.

'I want to talk to you.'

His fingers were tracing a pattern on the steering-
wheel—those long, slender, *loving* fingers . . . There was
a tight knot in her chest; she could hardly breathe.

'I don't want to talk to you,' she said finally. 'I want—I
want to collect my car.'

'But you see, *I* want to talk to *you*.'

'And so, of course, that's all that matters, isn't it?' she
burst out wildly. But she knew that he would not release
her until he was quite ready, so, with a great effort, she
managed to say more calmly, 'Well, go on then—what is
it?'

'I'll ask you again. Just where do you think you're
going?' Most of the anger had gone from his voice and he
sounded strained.

'I've told you, I was going to get my car.'

She shot him a fleeting sideways look, willing him to
turn to her, but his eyes were fixed on the scene before

them, his face aloof, even forbidding, so she went on huskily, 'Don't worry, Luke, I can take a hint. Thank you for looking after——'

'Take a hint?' He turned his head towards her sharply. 'What the hell do you mean? Look, Catherine, for God's sake don't play games with me any more.'

He spoke harshly, so that she quailed slightly before his anger. 'W-when I woke up this morning and you—weren't there——' she stared straight ahead, at a tiny whirlpool in the muddy water '—well, I realised the truth.' She stopped, momentarily quite unable to go on.

'And what the devil do you mean by that?' Luke gave an angry exclamation, then banged his fist against the steering-wheel. 'No—don't tell me. Let me guess. You thought that I regretted this morning, I suppose—that I never wanted to set eyes on you again?'

'Well, you knew I was leaving today. And when you weren't even there to say goodbye . . .' Her voice trailed away miserably. Oh why didn't he just start the car, take her to the garage, put an end to all this?

'If it comes to that, you didn't exactly hang around.' She stared at him, startled, and he laughed bitterly. 'As soon as my back was turned you were off—back to St Hilaire, no doubt, like a homing pigeon.'

Catherine licked her dry lips, then said uncertainly, 'Where were you then?'

'If you must know, I had another phone call from that blasted Linda. She really went over the top this time. Hysterics, actually threatening suicide. Much as I might have been tempted to leave her to it,' his voice was hard, 'I couldn't take the risk. I tore back upstairs, but you were still dead to the world. I thought I could safely leave you to sleep till lunch time. I dashed over to her place, to find that Roger, poor devil, has found out that for the past year she's been having a torrid affair with his business partner and he's now threatening to break every bone in her silly little body, and his partner's too, I gather.' He sounded grimly amused. 'I had a rather hairy session calming her down, then I raced back, only to find that you and your baggage had disappeared into thin air. I suppose I should be grateful that your sense of direction is every bit as shaky as I'd expect, or I might never have been able to tell you.'

'Tell me what?'

There was a faint tremor in her voice and he took her cold hands in his.

'Why, that I love you, of course.'

This wasn't happening—it couldn't be. Very slowly, Catherine turned her head towards him, to find his eyes on her, his face not angry but warm, his grey eyes full of a tenderness that she could never have imagined.

'But—but you don't love me,' she faltered.

'Don't love you?' He raised his dark brows in a meaningful look. 'And just what do you think that session in the guest-room was all about?'

She blushed. 'I thought—well, that you just wanted me.'

He bent his head and dropped a light, caressing kiss on the back of her hand, then looked up at her with a smile that made her feel light-headed, as though she had been drinking champagne.

'So I do, my darling girl. I want you so much I can hardly breathe, hardly live for wanting you.' He stroked his thumb softly across her wrist. 'It started that very first time on Coral Strand. I was locked in some very— unpleasant thoughts,' his eyes darkened for a moment, 'then I looked up, and this lovely, *glowing* girl was standing over me. Every time I met you I had to fight against my attraction more and more—after all, you were the girl whose beach we wanted, and I was the man who was never, but never going to trust a woman again! My surly beach-bum act was a great help, of course, but even so, it was a terrible struggle.

'That afternoon in your aunt's garden, I deliberately—

cruelly—set out to prove that I didn't love you, that it was only sexual desire. I told myself that it was just a stupid, rebound infatuation for a pretty girl who was as greedy and unprincipled as my wife had been. But then, when I was ill, I left your house because the ache of wanting to snatch you up and hold you to me was worse than all the ache of the fever. And when you told me about your parents—well, I had to get out fast or I'd have forgotten my promise to Steve and called the whole charade off there and then.'

'But at the airport——'

'At the airport, I *willed* you to come to me—I had to know if you loved me. I was watching as you parked your car. You were—beautiful, in your blue-green dress. You hadn't seen me, but then, as I moved towards you, Nick Alvarez appeared. I could have killed you both on the spot—he for being so undeserving of such a prize, and you for leading me on.' He saw her face. 'What's the matter?'

She said unsteadily, 'It was *you* I'd come to find. Nick—he just happened to be coming in on that flight.'

The sadness, those wasted months, those days and nights of heartbreak—they had all been unnecessary, after all. Luke's hand tightened painfully on hers and they stared at each other, the faint shadow of that desolation still in their eyes.

'But wasn't there anything between you and Nick? All the gossip in the Lord Nelson—I really thought——'

'Oh, there was once, light-years ago.' Catherine smiled gently. 'But that was just a silly teenage crush.'

'Well, I'd convinced myself that you were going to waste yourself, throw yourself away on that—good-for-nothing. That was why I tried desperately not to show you, much less tell you, how I felt, even out on the cay. And anyway, after the appalling way I'd treated you——' His tone was light enough, but his face showed for an instant some of the old strain. 'So you weren't hightailing it back to Nick's loving arms this morning?'

'Well,' her eyes sparkled with mischief, 'I don't think he would exactly greet me with open arms—and neither would his wife. Oh, yes,' she went on as he stared at her in astonishment, 'I forgot to tell you last night. Nick was married, oh, a couple of months ago now. Well,' she grinned at him impishly, 'don't you want to know who the lucky lady is?'

'You don't mean? Good lord, not *Mandy*?'

'Yes—Mandy.'

He laughed. 'Well, well. I'm sure they'll be very happy!' He paused, then went on more seriously, 'But what I can't understand is how on earth a mercenary devil like Alvarez could pass up the chance to marry an heiress.'

'Easy.' Catherine smiled at him and leaned back in her seat. The last vestiges of pain and sorrow were loosening their grip, gradually floating away, leaving only a delicious warmth. 'He never had the chance to pass me up and besides—I meant to tell you earlier, but I forgot—I'm not an heiress. No—it's true. You see, there was an election—oh, soon after you left. That's why Uncle Bob was in such a hurry, but he wasn't quick enough. The new government immediately banned all speculative land sales, the Coral Strand deal was axed and the government took it over.'

'What? Just like that? Wasn't there any compensation?'

'Oh, yes.' She smiled at the memory. 'I got what Dad originally paid for it—all six hundred dollars. Less expenses, of course.'

'But—couldn't you fight it?'

'I don't think so. Even Uncle Bob's resigned to it! It was a blow at first for us, I don't mind admitting. But now that Cinnamon House is doing so well, he's got over it. He's even talking of building another half-dozen bungalows and giving up his law practice to run them— not that Aunt Lu's very keen on that idea! And as for me, well, I've got over far worse than that, Luke. What I do regret, though,' her face clouded, 'I had planned to spend some of the money on a mothers' room at the hospital, and I was sorry about that. But otherwise——'

Luke put up his hand and gently brushed it across her face. 'My poor love, how I've misjudged you—wronged you.' His voice was unsteady. 'Forgive me please, my darling.'

Catherine smiled at him, then, feeling her whole body vibrant with love, she took his hand and kissed it softly.

He gave a sudden exclamation. 'Heavens, I'd almost forgotten. I'm supposed to be seeing my parents for lunch.' He ran his hands through his hair. 'Still—all the better. I'll take you—it's time they met their new daughter-in-law!'

She sat quite still. It was almost too much—she felt dizzy.

'What's the matter?' he asked.

She swallowed nervously. 'Nothing. Well—I was just wondering if they'll like me.'

'Like you?' He smiled at her in a way that made her knees tremble. 'My own darling, you're what they've been waiting for since the day I was born. But before we go—I'll show you the beach.'

As he locked the car, he said casually, 'By the way, is fifty thousand enough?'

'Fifty thousand?' She looked at him, puzzled.

'Pounds—for your mothers' room. A sort of early wedding-present, if you like—and a private thank you to St Hilaire for giving me you.'

She put her hands on his shoulders then, standing on tiptoe, brought his head down and kissed him, gently at first, then, as the kiss deepened, she clung to him until he drew back and they stared into each other's eyes, each intently seeking, and giving, the reassurance that each craved of the other. At last, Luke broke the almost unbearable tension with a shaky laugh, picking her up

and whirling her round him before letting her slide slowly
down his body. He dropped a quick kiss on her brow.

'Come on.'

He seized her hand and together they ran along a
footpath which wound beside the creek. Ahead was a
line of low sand dunes, dotted with coarse grass and the
silver spiked leaves of sea holly. Still hand in hand, they
mounted the crest of a dune, then Luke scrambled down
on to the sand and swung Catherine down beside him.
Breathless and laughing, she leaned against him.

The beach was a long, wide curve of creamy sand,
stretching as far as she could see in each direction, and
beyond was the sea, a thin, swaying silver line. As she
watched, the sun came out from behind a cloud and it
was as if the whole scene—beach, sea and sky—became
a huge, pearly opalescent globe of light.

'Like it?' Luke was watching her face.

Catherine nodded. 'It's beautiful, Luke—really beautiful.' She took a deep breath, revelling in the clean tang of
the salty air.

'And you won't miss—your life in St Hilaire?'

She saw the crease of worry between his brows, the set
line of his lips. 'What is it——?' she began, then stopped.
She understood his fear. She took his hands in hers and
said slowly, 'I'd be lying, Luke, if I said I'd never miss the
island. After all, it was my home for ten years. But it was
nothing to me in the end, without you.' She shook his
hands in emphasis and smiled. 'You know, I think Aunt
Lu realised that before I did.'

'And we can go back there often,' he said. 'I know how
much Hope's Mill means to you.'

'Yes, and I couldn't bear to see Mattie turned out—
she's been there for so long. She came as my nanny, you
know, and I've always been very close to her.' She lifted
her head and smiled up at him lovingly. 'That's what
she's always liked best—being a nanny, I mean. So, when
we go to stay there . . .'

Luke squeezed her to him convulsively, until she could hardly breathe. 'And yet, you always seemed so—right there, somehow. I didn't want you to feel trapped—far away from your beloved island.'

And you were afraid that one day I, too might run away, back to it, she added silently, but she only smiled at him.

'There's only one place I want to be, Luke, and you know that that's with you.' She took another deep breath and, loosing his hands, stood with arms outstretched, as though to embrace the whole lovely scene. A great sense of peace was washing through her body, easing away all unhappiness, all sorrows.

'I feel—oh, I feel as though I've come home,' she said, turning to him, and Luke, catching his breath at the sight of her radiant face, snatched her to him.

'I can't share you just yet. I'll ring my parents—tell them we'll be across for supper instead,' he said into her hair.

'Hey, that reminds me,' said Catherine. 'You promised Mrs Barnes you'd get my breakfast—and I'm ravenous.'

'Mmm, all right. I'll get you your breakfast—in bed, of course! And afterwards——' his voice was a murmur in her ear, so that she shivered deliciously '—afterwards, well——'

The wind stirred, whipping some of the fine sand against their faces and a pair of oyster-catchers wheeled and dipped over their heads.

'Come on,' Luke whispered softly. 'Let's go home.'

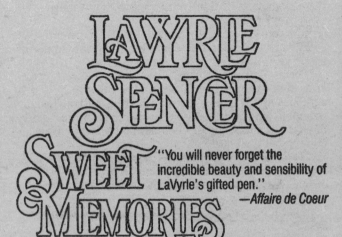

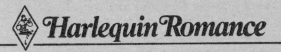

Harlequin Romance

Coming Next Month

Available in July wherever paperback books are sold, or through Harlequin Reader Service:

In the U.S.
901 Fuhrmann Blvd.
P.O. Box 1397
Buffalo, N.Y. 14240-1397

In Canada
P.O. Box 603
Fort Erie, Ontario
L2A 5X3